WHAT THE WIND PICKED UP

Other Collections by ChiLibris

The Storyteller's Collection: Tales of Faraway Places
The Storyteller's Collection, Book Two: Tales from Home

WHAT THE WIND PICKED UP

Proof that a Single Idea Can Launch a
Thousand Stories

From the Novelists of ChiLibris

iUniverse, Inc.
New York Lincoln Shanghai

What the Wind Picked Up
Proof that a Single Idea Can Launch a Thousand Stories

iUniverse books may be ordered through booksellers or by contacting:

iUniverse
2021 Pine Lake Road, Suite 100
Lincoln, NE 68512
www.iuniverse.com
1-800-Authors (1-800-288-4677)

This is a work of fiction. Names, characters, places, and incidents are either the product of the authors' imagination or are used fictitiously.

ISBN: 0-595-34113-6

Printed in the United States of America

Contents

What is ChiLibris?

The novelists' group known as ChiLibris began on a hot Sunday afternoon in July 1999. Twenty-five novelists gathered for lunch during a Christian booksellers' convention and had such a grand time together they decided to keep in touch via the Internet. Since that quiet beginning, the group has grown to more than 140 Christian novelists, all of whom are multi-published.

The members of ChiLibris communicate primarily through the Internet, but once a year we retreat for two days. During our retreat we learn, worship, and pray together. We share ideas and dreams and we have a *lot* of fun.

During the summer of 2004, we met in Atlanta. A small group of us went out for dinner, and as we discussed writing and work, the conversation turned to writer's conferences. Several of our members are writing instructors, and someone mentioned that beginning writers are often reluctant to share their work because they're afraid someone will steal their idea.

We chuckled, remembering when we used to fear the same thing. But since our fledgling days, we've learned that the *idea* isn't always the most important thing—how you *express* that idea is what matters. In fact you can't copyright an idea, only its expression.

On a whim, we decided to undertake an experiment—we would offer our group several particular building blocks and observe how different writers used them to build distinctly different stories.

Jeff Gerke (aka Jefferson Scott), provided our common elements:

Each writer's story had to begin with this unspectacular first line: *The wind was picking up.*

Each short story had to include a case of mistaken identity, a pursuit at a noted landmark, and an unusual form of transportation. We heard that Hitchcock used these three elements to create the wonderful film, *North by Northwest*. If he could rise to the challenge, so could we—and with far fewer words!

Finally, each story had to end with *So that's exactly what she did.*

We've had a lot of fun with our creations and we hope you will, too. Consider them twenty-one variations on a common theme. Enjoy the different genres of our authors and celebrate their unique voices. I think you'll especially enjoy the "writing advice" section that our novelists have contributed. If I'd had access to this wisdom when I started writing, my career path would have been a lot smoother.

As an added plus, know that your purchase of this book is helping others. All royalties from *What the Wind Picked Up* will go to Samaritan's Purse, a nondenominational evangelical Christian organization providing spiritual and physical aid to hurting people around the world. The organization serves the Church worldwide to promote the Gospel of the Lord Jesus Christ.

One more thing—the novelists of ChiLibris would like to thank (and hug the stuffing out of) Kirk DouPonce from Dog-Eared Design for graciously (and freely!) doing our awesome cover.

Ready to read? Settle back in your favorite chair and enjoy a few minutes with some of my dearest friends.

—Angela Elwell Hunt

Burl's Gift

Karen Ball

The wind was picking up.

Dog huddled closer to the building, shivering, empty belly aching. The concrete surface offered little shelter from the biting wind.

The sound came to her then. Jingling. It filled her weary heart with longing.

Peeking from where she hid, she saw it. A *stroller,* humans called it. Their young rode in them, pushed by mothers and fathers as they rushed along. But this stroller held no human.

What rode in this stroller was the source of the treasured jingling. An Owned Dog. Little. Furry. Proud. Neck adorned with a band holding tags. Tags meant a name. Tags meant belonging.

And tags jingled.

The Owned Dog looked at her and one lip curled. Before Dog could look away, show she meant no harm, the little dog lunged from the stroller, flying at Dog.

"Misty!"

Dog ran. She could stop, bite the Owned Dog in half, but its human was right behind it. Yelling. Angry.

Dog scrambled up stairs, the Owned Dog on her heels.

"Misty! No! Come *back* here!"

Feet jumped out of Dog's way. Human feet.

Human feet were bad. Worse than human voices. Those were loud. Angry. But she could run from voices. Human hands swatted, hit. Just as they tried to do now, grabbing at her. But she could snap at hands. Stop them. Make them pay.

Human feet didn't stop. They kicked. Bruised.

Dog curled her lips. Showed her fangs. Let the feet know.

Stay away.

More human voices, more yelling.

"Lady, what are you *doing?* Dogs aren't allowed in the Smithsonian!"

"*That's* my dog. That other *creature* is just some filthy stray! *Catch* it!"

Dog ducked another pair of hands and pushed past feet, slipped through an opening. Suddenly her paws were slipping, sliding.

"Look out! They just waxed the floors!"

Dog hurtled too fast to stop, slammed into something hard.

She yelped. Then spun around, snarling. Feet were everywhere. The stupid Owned Dog was caught, bound in its human's arms. And still it yapped. What did it have to yap about? Dog was the one in trouble.

"Stay back. Just leave it alone until we get animal control in here."

❦   ❦   ❦

Human feet and voices hovered everywhere. Dog pushed back against the hard wall.

Don't hurt. Don't—

She froze.

A human drew close. Holding out a long stick. She narrowed her eyes, let her low growl ask what the human wanted.

"Take it easy, fella."

This voice wasn't angry, but dog didn't care. Even when voices made her tail wag, the hands hit. Feet kicked.

Dog let her growl go deeper, showed more fang. *Stay away. Stay—*

"Hey, isn't that dog on one of the posters at the shelter?" *Another* human. Dog's hair bristled. "The one they're offering a reward for?"

"I don't know, Pete. That dog looked friendly. This dog looks…possessed."

"Whatever. Just distract it so I can snag it with the control pole."

Dog cowered, but there was no cover. Something looped over her head, snagged on her neck. She snapped and snarled, twisted, but it wouldn't let go. The large human held a stick attached to the loop. It pulled Dog. No matter how she fought, she couldn't escape. Couldn't stop the humans from dragging her. Lifting.

Pushing her into a cage.

Dog snarled. Screamed. She knew what cages meant.

She would not get free. Not ever.

The door closed.

Dog circled. Circled. Then curled into a ball at the back corner of the cage. Covered her face with her tail.

And cried.

❦   ❦   ❦

"I don't know, Burl. I doubt this one's gonna get adopted."

Burl Winters peered into the kennel, staring at the ratty dog cowering in the corner. "Not comin' 'round?"

"Can you believe Frank and Pete thought this was the dog on that poster?"

Burl scratched his head. "Well, it *kinda* looks like that dog."

"Burl. The dog on the poster is a black Lab. That look like a black Lab to you?"

Hardly. Okay, so this dog was mostly black and roughly the size of a Lab, but there were splotches of brown and white in its coat. And that coarse hair was pretty good evidence of some kind of terrier in the mix.

"Anyway," Jim went on, "someone did a real number on this animal. Too bad, too. I'm betting there's a nice dog under all that fear, for someone with lots of time and patience." He gave Burl a sideways glance. "Someone like you."

"Me? No thanks. Don't need a dog. Don't want one. Don't even like dogs that much."

"You don't, huh?" Jim's skepticism creased his brow. "Then why do you come here everyday to help out?"

Burl shrugged. "Beats watchin' soap operas." He peered at the dog again. "Ugly critter, isn't it?"

Jim was one of those shelter workers who loved anything with fur and four legs. "There's no such thing as an ugly dog."

"Well then—" Burl pointed with the handle of his mop—"put an ad in the paper! We got ourselves a rare, one-of-a-kind dog up for adoption. 'Cuz *that* animal is ugly. Cow pattie ugly, at that."

Jim shook his head and walked away. But his muttered words drifted back to Burl. "I don't know why I even try talking to you..."

Funny. Ethel used to say the same thing. 'Course, she never stopped trying. Not to the day she died.

He turned back to the empty kennel he was cleaning, gave a few final swipes with the mop, then grabbed up the bucket. Ugly Mutt was next. That's what he'd named the newest addition to the shelter, though he hadn't told anyone. Except, of course, the dog.

"Okay, Ugly. Your turn." He pulled the control pole off the wall, easing the latch on the dog's kennel. "You gonna try to take my arm off today?"

Every evening for the past two weeks, their dance had been the same. Burl opened the kennel door, talking low and gentle, control pole at the ready. Ugly Mutt tried to shove herself even farther back into the corner, snarling like a polecat. Burl eased the loop over the dog's head and Ugly Mutt launched, snapping like a demon. From there it was ease back out of the kennel, the dog-cum-Tasmanian-Devil on the pole, put her in an empty kennel, clean her kennel out, then start over again to get her back in her spot.

Lots of shelters would have put a dog like Ugly Mutt down. But this place was different. They did everything they could to rehab animals and find them homes. That's why Burl wanted to work here.

He believed in second chances. Even third and fourth chances.

Unfortunately, he thought as he closed Ugly Mutt into an empty kennel and watched her slink into the corner, sometimes there weren't enough chances in the world.

And that was a darned shame. Because if Ethel had taught him anything, it was that everyone—man or beast—had something inside them worth loving.

"Course some of us," he said, crouching down, trying to catch Ugly Mutt's eye, "bury it deeper than others. But it's there."

The dog growled and Burl's lips twitched.

"Somewhere."

Fifteen minutes later, he did the dance in reverse. By the time Ugly Mutt was finally ensconced back in the corner of her kennel, they were both exhausted. Burl stood there, looking down at the miserable animal. He started to turn away, then hesitated. Ugly Mutt was looking at him. She'd never done that before. She'd always avoided eye contact.

But there she lay, head on her paws, eyes fixed on him.

Bawling.

It didn't make sense, but there it was. Big ol' tears running out of those brown eyes, seeping into her fur. He knelt again, hand on the kennel door. If he didn't know better, he'd swear he knew the look in that dog's eyes. He'd seen it too often in his own reflection to miss it.

The look of a broken heart.

❦　　　❦　　　❦

Let me go.

Dog lay in the freshly cleaned concrete cage, head on her paws, weeping. Pleading. *Please, let me go.*

The human stayed, watching. His voice, soft and tail pleasing, kept speaking. And for once, Dog was not afraid. There was no room for afraid.

Only for sad.

She tried to make the human understand. To tell him there was no sky here. No moon. No sun. The scents were human and false and harsh. Sharp. Burning. No sweet grass, no fragrant refuse, no breeze carrying promise of delights to be foraged. Even the food was wrong. Soft. Without form.

Yes, she ate it. Dog knew better than to turn away from food. But there was no joy in the eating.

Please…do not keep me in the cage.

Burl listened to the animal's piteous whines, and felt tears prick at his own eyes. Without giving himself a chance to reconsider, he reached up, opened the latch on the door, and stepped inside the kennel.

Sure, it was foolish. He didn't care.

He took a step forward and the dog lifted her head, watching him. But she didn't snarl. Didn't growl. Just kept those wide, grieving eyes on him.

"I know, girl. Believe me, I know. It wasn't that long ago I laid on my bed, crying out, begging someone to make things better." He drew a shaky breath. "But t'weren't no way to do that. She was gone."

Ethel. He could still see her face so clear. Hear her voice.

Another step closer. "You know, I only loved one woman all my life. And I swear, when she left this world—" he stood beside the dog now—"she took my heart with her."

Tears slid free as he knelt beside the animal, forced words out of his choked throat. "The day she died, I knew. Things would never be better again."

Dog listened. The human's voice spoke her heart. She heard it. Her own weeping was in his mouth. Her sorrow was in his heart. She felt it as he drew close.

For the first time in Dog's life, there was no fear. No fight.

Only that which they shared.

She crawled closer to him, her belly rubbing on the cold concrete. She lifted a paw, laid it on his leg.

He sat beside her, lifted a hand—a large, human hand—and lay it on her head. She tensed, ready for a blow. Ready to retreat. But the hand stroked her head. Caressed her ears.

His voice came again. So sad. So sad.

"I miss her, Ugly Mutt. Every day, I miss her."

His hand held only kindness. Dog closed her eyes. She had felt this touch before. Soft. Gentle. Her mother's tongue when Dog was a puppy. Warm with care and love.

Dog sighed, laying her head on the human's leg.

She missed her mother.

❦   ❦   ❦

Burl wasn't sure how long he sat there, Ugly Mutt's head resting on his leg, his hand on her scruffy head, scratching her uneven, flopped ears. Time was irrelevant in the face of mutual peace and comfort.

Not until his old bones started to protest did he admit he'd have to get up off the concrete floor. He didn't want to. Would have been just as happy to stay there. But he had more work to finish. Other dogs needed their areas cleaned, and he couldn't forget that. He gave the dog a final pat, then stood.

She stood, too, standing beside him, looking up at him with those eyes. He laid his hand on her head. "I'll be back."

❦   ❦   ❦

And so he was. Day after day.

Each evening, Ugly Mutt watched with quiet patience as he cleaned the kennels. When it was her turn, she walked with him to the holding kennel until her area was cleaned. Then they both moved back to her kennel, to sit and talk together. One night Burl came in with a nice, soft dog cushion.

Jim, who was getting ready to leave, looked first at the cushion, then at Burl. "You're crazy, you know that?"

"Why, just 'cuz I bring a dog a cushion?"

"No," Jim replied on a chuckle, "because you bring her toys and biscuits and a blanket and a food dish. *And* a cushion." He pulled on his jacket. "I swear, Burl, why don't you just admit what we all know."

Burl pursed his lips. "Which is?"

"That dog is yours. She lays there all day until she hears you coming. Then she's up on her feet, watching for the first sight of you. And you're just as bad. She's all you talk about any more." He shook his head. "Give it up, bud. Admit you're hooked, bring her the only thing you haven't bought her yet—a collar and a license—and take the animal home."

Burl stood there, watching as Jim walked away. Then he turned and went to Ugly Mutt's kennel. She sat there, tail wagging, gladness shining in those dark eyes, her furry face lit in a doggie smile...

Burl spun on his heel and marched back to the reception area. "Jean, I'm leaving."

Before the woman could ask him any questions, he went outside to his car, threw the dog cushion in the trunk, and slipped in behind the steering wheel. His fingers trembled on the key as he slid it into the ignition.

Take Ugly Mutt home? Let her depend on him. Love him. Maybe even come to love her?

No.

Love meant losing.

Losing meant pain.

He'd had his fill of both.

Turning the key in the ignition, he gunned the engine and drove from the parking lot like his life depended on it.

❦   ❦   ❦

Dog waited.

The false light was gone and darkness covered the cage. But still she waited. Her human would come. He would come.

Earlier, she'd heard his step, smelled his scent. Had seen him for just a moment. But he turned and left. And as he did, she caught a new scent from him.

Fear.

Dog knew fear. Fear could be good. It could save your life.

Or, if it was bad fear, end it.

Worry. Sadness. They nagged at Dog, making her pant hard and fast. She fixed her eyes on the big hole where her human usually came in, smiling and talking to her. How she wished he were here now. His voice always made her feel better. Safe.

Loved.

Dog let her eyes close. Let her mind bring back the sound of her human's voice. The touch of his hand on her head.

A sound made her jump. Open her eyes. Stare...

And suddenly she was dancing. Wiggling from head to toe. Tail wagging, a proud flag of her devotion.

He was here!

She watched him walk to her cage. Let her ears rejoice as he talked in the only human voice she'd ever loved.

"Okay, you ugly mutt. I've had it. You waltz in here, make everyone miserable, and then just think you can force your way into my life."

Dog watched, joy making her paws prance as he opened the kennel door and knelt next to her. He took hold of her head, and Dog froze. He was putting something around her neck! Fear skittered down her spine.

Fight! Bite him! Run away! He's going to hurt you, just like all the other humans have hurt you before!

But Dog didn't do it. This was her human. And his voice told her fear was lying.

"Well, guess what?" His hands held her neck still, secured it with something. "You're absolutely right."

Dog heard happy in his voice. She shook her head and heard another sound, too.

Jingling.

Her human reached out, cupped the tags now hanging at her neck.

She was owned! Dog couldn't keep the happy inside. She danced and spun and licked her human's face.

"Okay, girl, okay!" Her human's laughter was a sweet sound. "There's just one problem. Ain't no way *my* dog is gonna be named Ugly Mutt. So from now on, if it's okay with you, your name is *Dotty.*" His hands stroked her head, tickled her ears. "Know what that means? *A gift from God.* I think that fits pretty well, don't you?"

Crying was in his eyes, but Dog didn't worry. Because he was smiling. She licked his face, his hand. He hugged her close, then stood.

"Okay, Dotty, know what I think?"

She sat, looking up at him, content to be at his side. *Just tell me. Tell me what you want me to do.*

"I think it's time you came home."

Dog didn't hesitate. Her human loved her. He wanted her to go home.

So that's exactly what she did.

*   *   *

KAREN BALL, author, editor, and speaker, has more than twenty years of experience in publishing. Her novels include the best-selling *The Breaking Point, A Test of Faith, Wilderness,* and *Reunion* (all Multnomah). *Shattered Justice,* the first book in Karen's new The Family Honor series, will be out in July 2005. As an editor, Karen has had the honor of working with such notable novelists as Francine Rivers, Terri Blackstock, Karen Kingsbury, Liz Curtis Higgs, Angela Hunt, Bill Myers, Robin Lee Hatcher, Robin Jones Gunn, and Gilbert Morris. Karen lives in Oregon with her husband, Don, and their "ids," a mischief-making Siberian named Bo and an irrepressible blue-eyed Aussie-Terrier mix named "Dakota."

Hero

James Scott Bell

The wind was picking up.

Garth Himmelfarb headed right into it. This was his first night out on a new exercise regimen—brisk walk around the mall, then home—but he was already feeling fatigue.

Push on, big guy, he thought. Then, patting his ample, forty-five year-old gut, said out loud, "You're goin' down!"

In truth, he held little hope of that. Garth Himmelfarb had started and stopped more diets and body-improvement programs than he could shake a Slim-Fast at. Every one of them went down in flaming defeat. In recent years his wife had gone from motivator to nag about it. She had started saying things like, "I just don't find you that attractive anymore" and "I never wanted to be married to a man with a paunch!"

That had led to Garth's increased drinking, and alcohol was not conducive to reducing the old tum tum.

Now, huffing and puffing across a major intersection, Garth realized he was in the middle of a dispiritingly familiar pattern.

First, he would get inspired. This time it had happened while watching an old Tarzan movie starring Johnny Weissmuller. Garth loved old movies, and especially the Weissmuller Tarzan flicks. No one could do the Tarzan yell like Weissmuller. And man, did that guy look good in a loincloth! Garth had been a swimmer when he'd met Chloe, and one of the things she fell for was his smooth, svelte body. So seeing Tarzan flying on the vines got his blood boiling to try reducing again.

The second part of the pattern was that Chloe was gone. Back east to visit her sister. At least a week. Garth always started these things when his wife was away because he wanted to surprise her. She'd come back and see not Garth

Himmelfarb, but Rex the Jungle King. And animal passions would be reawakened.

Third, he'd try to peel off months of corpulence right out of the chute. Inevitably he'd end up with a pulled muscle and sore knees.

Finally, he'd see the futility of it all and buy a box of Dove bars.

Well, tonight would be different! He would make it so! Yes, tonight the world would see the new Garth Himmelfarb, master of his own fate!

He stumbled over a crack in the sidewalk.

But he recovered, and as he turned the corner around the mall, which was just a couple of blocks from his suburban home, Garth felt the first surge of rebellion in his legs. His muscles were lighting fires in his calves and thighs.

Oh no, he thought. Not so soon!

He tried to think of Johnny Weissmuller again, but Tarzan had disappeared into the jungle of Garth's discomfort. He needed fresh inspiration, but where would he find it?

That's when he saw Jennifer Lopez.

She was walking past the Blockbuster that was at the northwest corner of the mall, dressed in a form flattering blouse, tight jeans, and thick-soled sandals that made a clacking sound when she walked.

And she was walking fast, in the same direction as Garth, who kept his eye on her from the sidewalk.

Jennifer Lopez! Do I dare say something?

But then he thought, *What is Jennifer Lopez doing in my neighborhood?*

He walked faster. If it wasn't J-Lo, it was sure someone who had the same goods.

A bit faster he walked, thinking, *And if it's not J-Lo, maybe she's someone I could talk to…*

The girl quickened her step.

So did Garth.

Suddenly she took a left turn, past the travel agency, and headed off toward Target on the other side of the parking lot.

And that was that. Garth knew he would never see her again unless he followed her. And even he was not that big a fool. All he needed was some jealous boyfriend bopping him one. He kept right on walking toward the next corner.

It took him nearly fifteen minutes of increasing misery to circumnavigate the mall. By the time he got to the crossing that would take him back to his neighborhood, he was thinking about how good those Dove bars would taste. And Chloe wasn't there to say a darn thing about it! Sweet relief.

At the signal Garth pressed the button and waited for the light to change. Then he looked to his left and saw her.

The girl was punching the crossing button on the other side. There was a desperation about her actions, as if she were hurrying away from something.

Garth couldn't stop looking at her, wondering what her story was. He wished she were on his side of the street, so he might casually ask—

The light changed. The girl took off across the intersection. So did Garth, watching her the entire time.

On the other side was the start of the residential section. Not as many streetlights here. The night was moonless and quiet.

Garth could hear the clacking of the girl's shoes on the opposite sidewalk. They were now virtually side-by-side across the ribbon of street, walking at the same pace.

Then Garth saw the girl cast a quick glance his way. All of a sudden she started to run, slowly and clumsily in her big shoes, but desperately, as if the sight of him had made her afraid.

Garth wanted to shout at her not to be afraid. But who could blame her? In these times? Dark night, nobody out, girl walking alone, fat guy following her. Any sane girl would feel a trickle of fear.

He spoke to her in his mind. *Hey, you don't have to be scared. You're a pretty girl and I'm just a guy walking and…*he stopped himself, for a dangerous picture was forming in his mind. It was a picture of him and this girl, alone in his house, about to do something that would shock the life out of Mrs. Himmelfarb.

The girl was now half a block ahead of Garth. The *clack-clack* of her shoes slowed as she settled into a walk again, albeit a fast one.

She kept looking behind her.

Garth found that his legs now had plenty of life in them. He was keeping up after her. It made no sense to do so, but he did anyway. She was a mystery. He wanted to solve her.

Another half a block and she was still walking fast. Garth became aware of headlights on the street and saw a Ford Bronco whiz past him, heading in the direction of the girl. Nothing strange about a car on the street.

What was strange was when the Bronco went a little way past the girl and stopped; it stopped in the middle of the street, as if waiting for her.

What was this? Some guy joy riding, seeing a pretty girl, stopping to toss out some pickup line?

Garth walked faster so he could take in the scene. The girl did not stop walking. If the person in the Bronco said anything to the girl she gave no indication that she heard it. Or cared to hear it.

The Bronco started up again and shot past the girl. Only this time it pulled over to the curb.

A man got out. He was short and thickset, a dark silhouette. He started across the street.

Toward the girl.

Garth's heart suddenly beat like he'd been running wind sprints. He could hear his pulse pounding like pistons in his ears.

What did this man intend to do?

What if, Garth wondered, he lays a hand on her? What should I do then?

What if the guy had a gun or something? What if he was a psycho?

Garth stopped just short of where the girl and the man were across the road. There was a conveniently placed eucalyptus tree for Garth to hide behind.

He watched as the two dark figures seemed to converse, then the girl made a move to try to walk away. The man stepped in front of her.

She said something Garth could not make out.

This was getting to the critical stage, Garth was sure. Soon he'd have to do something. But was he man enough?

Then, as quickly as he had come, the man walked back across the street to his Bronco, got in and drove toward the next corner.

The girl stood frozen.

Garth watched the taillights of the Ford turn the corner and disappear.

That's when Garth made his decision. He jogged—his legs carrying him with newfound energy—over to the girl. "Are you okay?"

She turned toward him. Garth stopped before he reached the curb. He didn't want her to think he was going to do anything to her. But he could see her face in the amber light of a lone streetlamp, and his breath shot out of him. She was the most stunningly beautiful girl he had ever seen.

"Eh?" she said.

"Are you all right?"

She shrugged.

"Did he try anything with you?"

"My husband." She had a mild Hispanic accent.

Husband? Now Garth felt the perfect fool. In all his imaginings, he had not hit on what was the most obvious scenario. This was a woman in a spat with her husband! She took off, he drove after her, they were having a family fight.

Great going, Garth.

"Oh," he said stupidly. "I'm sorry."

"No," she said. "I am afraid."

Afraid! So it was true. Her husband was a wife beater or something, maybe worse. And where was he? Circling the block? Waiting for her in the shadows of another street?

Garth thought quickly, then said, "Come with me."

The woman looked confused.

"I live just down this street," Garth said, indicating the next corner. "We can call the police."

"No police," she said.

"But you can't just let him—"

A set of headlights hit them and she jumped into him. Her body was trembling. The car that passed them was a Honda.

"I go with you."

"This way," Garth said.

They got to his house without anyone seeing them, so far as Garth could tell. He flicked on the lights and wished then he had cleaned up the place. He'd left the television on, because a local station was showing *Tarzan's New York Adventure,* one he hadn't seen.

At that very moment, Tarzan (the great Johnny Weissmuller!) was being chased by cops on top of some skyscrapers. He grabbed a flagpole rope and, using it like a jungle vine, swung to the next rooftop.

Garth thought this would be a good time to break the ice. "Look at that Tarzan go, huh?"

The woman said nothing, her face a blank.

The cops kept up the chase all the way to the Brooklyn Bridge. Tarzan saw them closing in and started climbing up the bridge!

Garth chuckled, hoping the woman would relax. "They'll never catch him."

No response.

Reluctantly, Garth switched off the TV. "Please sit."

The woman lowered herself into a soft chair. She breathed rhythmically. Garth thought for a moment he might pass out at the sight of her.

Her eyes were opals, hypnotic.

Her smooth skin looked softer than anything he had ever seen.

Her velvety black hair cascaded around her shoulders.

And Garth began to think *Maybe, just maybe.* After all, he had been like a knight in shining armor for her, hadn't he? She obviously was having trouble at home. The night was young and Chloe wasn't around and…

He noticed his hands were sweating. He wiped them on his shorts.

"Thank you," the woman said. Her accent made him think of Lupe Valez who, he remembered, had once been married to Johnny Weissmuller.

Me, Tarzan.

"Me…my name is Garth."

"I am Juana." And then she smiled. Was it his imagination, atrophied after all these years with Chloe, or was the flash of white teeth within those lips purposely seductive?

Garth's rational mind came roaring back. *Snap out of it! This is not some movie and you're not a jungle king! You have injected yourself into a family situation and now, buddy, you better find a way to eject right out of it.*

"There are places you can go," Garth said. "I mean, for women who are married to abusive husbands. I could make a call or two and—"

She shook her head. "No. I want to stay."

"Stay?"

"With you."

Garth's rational mind came crashing down like an old building under a wrecking ball.

"All right," he said.

She stood up then, not once taking her eyes off Garth's. He could not look away, like a snake being charmed. Only it was she who moved, swayed really, toward him. When she put her warm, soft hand on his cheek, he was lost. He knew it. He didn't care.

His arms shot out like coiled jungle cats. They wrapped around her body and he pulled her toward him.

Don't do it Garth! You're a married man! This is a sin, you fool!

Me Tarzan!

With his eyes closed he sought her mouth, then heard a clicking sound, like the flicking of a switch.

He opened his eyes.

A single hot flame flared under his ribs.

He staggered back, looked down, saw blood. It was pouring from his chest.

He looked up at the woman. She was watching him, eerily detached. In her right hand was a switchblade, dripping red.

Garth Himmelfarb cried out. His last thought on earth was that he didn't sound anything like Johnny Weissmuller.

❦   ❦   ❦

Detective Roger Owens shook his head at the pathetic figure of Esteban Cruz. The man sat weeping in the hard chair at Owens's desk, but the cop had no sympathy.

"Why didn't you report her before?" Owens said.

"I try to stop her. I try to talk to her, but she no listen to me! I stop her on the street, I get mad, I drive away."

"And how many times has she done this?"

Cruz shrugged. "Eight maybe?"

"You mean you don't *know* how many she's killed?"

"My wife, she no listen to no one. She's not right in her head, you know?"

"This is very serious for you, Mr. Cruz. Very serious. You should have come forward right away."

The poor man nodded. "I love her," he said. Then he looked at the detective pleadingly. "I try to stop her! I try!"

"You're a real hero," Owens said. Then he sighed at the familiar unfolding. Some fancy lawyer would take her case. He'd make a big emotional appeal to the jury. *She couldn't help herself! She had to kill! So that's exactly what she did!*

✳   ✳   ✳

JAMES SCOTT BELL is a winner of the Christy Award for Excellence in Christian Fiction. He has been featured in the *Los Angeles Times*, where his work was compared to John Grisham and Raymond Chandler. Among his best-selling novels are *Breach of Promise* (Zondervan) and the Kit Shannon series which began with *City of Angels* (Bethany House). Jim teaches novel writing at Pepperdine University and at writers' conferences across the country, and is the author of *Write Great Fiction: Plot & Structure* (Writers Digest Books). He and his wife Cindy are the parents of two college students, Nate and Allegra. When he's not writing Jim enjoys hanging out with his wife and teaching adult Bible studies at his church in Southern California. His website is www.jamesscottbell.com.

The Dubious Dinghy

Ron and Janet Benrey

The wind was picking up.

We were in the mouth of the Severn River, sailing east toward the Chesapeake Bay at a frightening speed, tilted to the right at a twenty-degree angle. I loosened the dinghy's mainsheet, but the little sailboat continued to dig its leeward rail into the water. James let out a Confederate war whoop and used his body like a counterweight to bring our sailboat back in balance.

He seemed completely at ease with his feet on the edge of the upwind rail and his body hanging way out over the Severn in an "impossible" position, supported only by a slender wire that ran between his vest-like harness and a fitting near the top of *Streak's* mast. "This rig is called a trapeze," James had explained back at the dock. "My fate is in your hands! Our sail today will be a perfect example of love-driven trust. You steer the sailboat; I ride the trapeze. If you goof, you'll drop me straight into the drink."

I looked at James hanging from the mast and pondered how my husband of less than a year had been able to talk me into crewing a "5-0-5" dinghy. His approach had been exceedingly clever.

"We need a wholesome activity we can do together," he'd said. "Something we both enjoy. We have to recognize that my consulting business and your headhunting firm are two different worlds."

"Do you have a suggestion?"

He beamed from ear to ear. "Dinghy racing in Annapolis Harbor on Wednesday evenings. We both love to sail. It'll be perfect. In fact, I've found the ideal sailboat for us."

I conceded that James had a point. The idea of a common hobby appealed to me as a way of merging our "different worlds." I am the proprietor of Philippa Hunnechurch & Associates, Executive Recruiters, while James is an international marketing consultant. Our respective businesses triggered what James calls our "last name compromise." I answer to Pippa Huston in Atlanta, where James hails from, and Pippa Hunnechurch in Ryde, Maryland, where we live and work. James has a wholly different set of clients and often travels; consequently we keep very different schedules. I could see a nugget of wisdom in James's observation that committing to race in Annapolis would force both of us to work extra hard to keep Wednesday evenings free.

"Dinghy racing? It sounds—ah—*challenging.*"

"It's easier than falling off the proverbial log! We'll be sailing a 5-0-5. I found a used boat in great shape at an irresistible price."

"A 5-0...*what?*"

"A small sailboat that's named for its length. Sixteen feet six inches works out to 5.05 meters. I skippered a 5-0-5 back in Georgia, on Lake Lanier. I was only fifteen at the time. It's an easy boat to drive."

He clinched the deal with, "The 5-0-5 was architected by one of your countrymen, Pippa. A Brit named John Westell designed the boat in the early 1950s. Tens of thousands have been built since then. It's a true classic."

Because James is an excellent salesperson, he never once uttered the phrase, "finicky racing machine." His slick sales pitch, coupled with my foolish belief that a man approaching the sagacious age of forty-five years would have gracious sensibilities, caused me to envision a charming mini yacht with an elegant hull, polished teak trim, soft seat cushions, a little cuddy cabin where one could stow a picnic hamper, and a comfortable cockpit where James's thirty-nine year old wife could enjoy a hot cuppa poured from a thermos.

That was the image in my mind when James led me to a no-frills vessel named *Streak* that had all the esthetic charm of a plastic sink. She had a gleaming white hull with an electric blue lightning bolt painted on each side. Everything in sight was made of plastic, aluminum, or stainless steel—and seemed purely utilitarian. No handy cup holders, no cozy cuddy cabin, and nary a splinter of decorative teak. *Streak* had absolutely no need for seat cushions because her so-called "seats" were the tops of her flotation chambers. In short, James' "ideal sailboat" seemed little more than a convenient float to hold the mast and sails.

"She's a real thoroughbred," he'd said proudly. "You'd have to search long and hard to find a faster boat of her size."

"Or a more wet one," I muttered to myself as a wave came over the side and washed my face all the way around my head. I spat out half a mouthful of water.

"This afternoon we'll merely get the feel of the boat," James had promised me at home. "The races don't begin until next month, so we won't do any serious sailing—just a little puttering around."

Everything had changed when James saw whitecaps on the water. "This is great!" he shouted. "If you think *Steak's* going fast today, wait until we learn how to rig the spinnaker."

The spinnaker is the big sail that looks like a stuffed shirt. It attaches to the front of a sailboat with a bewildering array of lines, and hardware, and poles. It seemed fiddly enough, thank you very much, to steer *Streak* with only her mainsail and jib hoisted. The thought of fussing with a spinnaker made me cringe.

"Whoo-ee!" James shouted. "We're planing!

I looked at the river racing past and realized that *Streak's* bow was at least a foot out of the water. Our 5-0-5 was on a plane, skimming along the surface like a surfboard or a high-performance motorboat.

"How fast are we going, James?"

"Oh…twelve or thirteen knots.

"Good grief! That's a nautical mile every five minutes. I've never traveled this fast in a sailboat."

"I can't hear you. I think the wind's picking up some more."

Blimey! More wind. Just what we need.

"Pippa!" he shouted at me. "Do you want to try riding the trapeze?"

"Don't be daft!"

On the bright side, James had assured me that the 5-0-5 was unsinkable. The worst that could befall us was an unceremonial dunking if—or when—the little boat went over. We were both wearing full-size lifejackets and the Severn River is an exceedingly busy body of water. We would get wet should disaster strike, but we weren't in peril.

Curiously, as our sail progressed, I began to doubt that disaster would strike. I found myself able to control *Streak* with surprising ease. She had an incredibly responsive tiller. A little twitch would alter our course and keep us in tune with the wind. I felt increasingly proud of my newly won skills.

Send the thought away, Pippa. Pride goes before a capsize, a haughty spirit before the splash.

James suddenly shouted. "That's got to be *Diablo*." He pointed at another 5-0-5, this one with a red hull, about two hundred yards off our port side. "Let's pay her a visit."

"Easier said than done," I muttered to myself.

One difficulty was that *Diablo* was headed back to Annapolis. We would have to turn *Streak* around—a tricky chore in heavy winds. Another problem was that *Diablo* was crewed by an experienced 5-0-5 team. It would be difficult to overtake them.

Diablo was owned by a couple in their early thirties who had been dinghy racing since childhood. We'd met Kevin and Michelle Wilson earlier that afternoon at the marina. Both were short and athletic and seemed a perfect fit for the compact 5-0-5.

James tapped my hand. "I hate to interrupt your musing, but *Diablo* is getting farther away every second. Kevin and Michelle seem an interesting couple. I think we should get to know them better."

In for a penny, in for a pound.

"Prepare to come about!" I shouted.

"Ready about," James shouted back.

I cautiously brought *Streak* into the wind. Our sails began to flap. James slid down into the shallow cockpit and managed to maneuver over my knees as the boom swung past his head. The sails filled as we settled on our new tack.

It may not have been the prettiest come-about in sailing history, but we didn't turn turtle, thanks mostly to James's surprising agility and balance.

"You missed your calling as a ballet dancer," I said.

"As a consultant, I'm frequently required to do fancy footwork."

"Very funny. However, I urge you to stop wasting your limited mental energy on silly puns and figure out how we can catch *Diablo*. Our hot pursuit seems doomed to failure because she's going faster than we are."

The wind was directly behind us now, so we didn't have any tipping forces to counteract. "For starters, I'll raise the centerboard," James said. "That will reduce unnecessary underwater drag. Next, I'll adjust the mainsail for optimum downwind sailing. Finally, we'll sail 'wing-on-wing.'"

"You must be bonkers!" I squeaked.

Sailing "wing-on-wing" meant having the mainsail extended to one side of the boat and the jib sail on the other. It would increase our effective sail area, but on a windy day a teensy steering error could cause an accidental "gybe" and make the boom swing across the boat like a rocket-propelled scythe.

"Have faith in yourself, Mrs. Hunnechurch-Huston." James gave me a big grin. "You're up to the task."

"You paid for the boat," I said with a moan. "Don't blame me if a bad gybe rips the boom off the mast."

I eased *Streak* into as stable a downwind point of sail as I could muster. The mainsail was on the starboard side of the boat. James tugged the jib sheets to bring our front sail to the port side. The sail filled with a loud *thump*.

Throughout the next ten minutes, I kept one eye on the little wind vane attached to the wire supporting the mast and the other on the sail, searching for any telltale flutter that would signal an impending gybe.

"You're doing great," James said. "We're definitely closing the gap."

I risked a quick glance away from the sail and saw that James was right. The distance between us had shrunk to about one hundred yards. *Streak* and *Diablo* were both running on a direct course for the U.S. Naval Academy. The big copper-covered dome of the Navy Chapel—one of the best-known landmarks in Annapolis Harbor—lay dead ahead. Its famous copper patina appeared an even richer green through my bronze-tinted sunglasses.

When I looked back at James, he was fiddling with the pair of lightweight binoculars he had bought especially for dinghy racing. When folded they were scarcely larger than his wallet and fitted nicely into his waterproof fanny pack.

"I guess this stops being a two-person boat when we're running before the wind." I hoped my voice dripped with sarcasm. "One of us seems to have nothing to do except look at the scenery."

James didn't reply. He'd directed all his attention to *Diablo*.

"Earth to James," I said. "Come in, please."

James seemed puzzled when he finally put down the binoculars. "We made a mistake. I thought we were following *Diablo*, but that's obviously a different boat. The guy in cockpit is wider across the back and bulkier in the shoulders than Kevin—and at least thirty pounds heavier." He added glumly, "The wind has died down. Let's stop wing-on-winging and head back to the marina."

I made a slight course correction to the left; James "gybed" the jib to *Streak's* starboard side.

"Can I have a look?"

"Sure." He took the tiller. I readjusted the binoculars and surveyed the dubious dinghy.

We were once again moving away from the red 5-0-5, but I had a perfect view of her hull. When she turned slightly I was able to read the name painted on her stern: *Diablo*. James's "mistaken identity" wasn't a mistake after all—although the couple in the cockpit did seem much too hefty to be Kevin and Michelle. They looked wider and bulkier, but also lumpier—an attribute that James hadn't mentioned.

"That's barmy," I muttered. "We saw them leave the dock."

And then I remembered that the Wilsons had been wearing t-shirts and shorts when we met them. *Diablo's* crew had donned seemingly oversized anoraks. Their outerwear explained their wider and bulkier appearance.

But not the lumpy look.

The penny dropped. I lowered the binoculars.

"See what I mean?" James said.

"Indeed I do, my love. A mistake was clearly made."

I made a spot decision not to share my conclusions with James. On the one hand, he doesn't like me to "play detective." On the other hand, a private word in the appropriate ear might save our budding friendship with the Wilsons, with James none the wiser.

I telephoned Michelle Wilson the next morning.

After the friendly niceties, I dove right in and explained what we'd seen in Annapolis Harbor. "Your extra-large anoraks convinced James that *Diablo* was another 5-0-5. But then James is a trusting soul who, like most men, tends to ignore the cut of clothing. I tend to be more skeptical, particularly when I see sharp-edged lumps."

Michelle tried to protest, but I kept talking.

"Your jumpers have weights stitched inside—and I figured out why. Neither you nor Kevin is heavy enough to do the kind of counterbalancing that I watched James do. So you decided to add poundage to your anoraks." I took a quick breath. "I'm not an expert on the rules of dinghy racing, but I believe that hiding weights in one's clothing is considered cheating.

"However, neither James nor the 5-0-5 race organizers will learn what I observed if you revise your racing strategy. I expect to see the Wilsons wearing dazzlingly svelte sailing jackets next Wednesday. I urge you to visit Fawcett's immediately and buy a pair."

I didn't give her a chance to argue, so that's exactly what she did.

*   *   *

RON & JANET BENREY have been a successful writing team since the late 1980s. They are best known for the Pippa Hunnechurch Mysteries, published by Broadman & Holman. The most recent of Pippa's murderous adventures—*Humble Pie*—was published in May 2004. Ron and Janet's latest thriller, *Dead as a Scone*, published by Barbour Publishing, is the first of their new Royal Tunbridge Wells Mysteries series. You can learn more about the

Benreys and their novels by visiting their web sites: www.benrey.com, www.pippahunnechurch.com, and www.teamuseum.org.

Reinventing Love

Stephen Bly

"The wind was picking up," she said.

Judge Hiram T. Young leaned toward the diminutive woman in the witness stand. "You shot your husband because the wind was picking up?"

She fussed at the high lace collar on her green gingham dress. "I hate the wind."

"Nebraska winds can aggravate to the point of distraction." The judge loosened his black narrow tie. "That doesn't justify attempted murder."

"I didn't try to murder him. I just wanted the wind to stop blowing."

A man with a badge stomped to the front of the courtroom. "The blast from a ten gauge Winchester 1887 shotgun is not tossing sunflowers to the wind. She shot him in the—"

"Sheriff, everyone in the county is aware of where she shot him." Judge Young glanced at the pocket watch that rested on a black Bible. "Now, madam, explain why the wind had anything to do with shooting your husband on June eleventh."

She rubbed her palms as if they were sore or cold. "June tenth."

The judge tapped the stack of papers. "The report states that Mr. Westclock was shot by Mrs. Westclock on June eleventh, 1892."

She stared at the thin man in ducking overalls. "He didn't know what day of the month it was."

"Don't start in with that again, Priscilla," the man shouted.

"Quiet." Judge Young slumped under a faded photograph of Benjamin Harrison.

"She almost killed me."

"Sit down, Mr. Westclock."

"I can't sit down."

"Then stand quietly."

"This isn't the first time, Your Honor. My life is in constant jeopardy," Mr. Westclock said.

The sheriff jammed his hands in his back pockets. "He claims she has attacked him with a pitchfork, axe handle, buggy whip, pitcher of hot milk and a fire poker."

"The fire poker was an accident." Her voice was as soft as a lullaby. "Never once did I have murder on my mind. I have no desire to raise my children alone."

The judge rubbed the back of his sweaty neck. "How many children do you have?"

"Nine," Mr. Westclock boomed.

"Eight," Mrs. Westclock corrected. "One of the twins died when all the babies got the flu that January." She stared across the room at the wide eyed children sitting silent on a hard wooden bench. "William, you were always gone when I gave birth, or the children fell ill."

"That's woman's work," he huffed.

Mrs. Westclock's thin face beamed. "Your Honor, these are our girls: Willie Jean is nine. She's holding the baby, Wallis, who is one. Then there's Weslina, eight; Wynona, seven; Wilma, six; Wendolyn, five; Wanetta, four; and Westalia, two."

"I was sick that one winter," Mr. Westclock explained.

"Mrs. Westclock, get back to the deeds of June tenth."

"We had thirty straight days without wind. William said that as soon as there was a strong wind, he would leave."

"Why was he waiting for a wind?"

She studied her short, dainty fingernails. "To push that thing of his."

"It's an Aereo-quad Land-Darter," Mr. Westclock announced.

"He took four bicycle wheels, mounted them to a wooden frame, then attached a windmill on top. He claims it is the vehicle of the future."

"The windmill pivots with the wind and drives gears that propel the Land-Darter," Mr. Westclock said. "I need to get to Denver to apply for a patent."

"What if the wind don't blow?" the sheriff asked.

"The two sets of pedals operate like a bicycle. I foresee concrete trails stretching from St. Louis to San Francisco and Aereo-quad Land-Darters dashing happy passengers in smooth silence as they arrive relaxed and refreshed to their destination."

"Was June tenth your test run?" the judge asked.

"I proved it when I took it for a spin around Chimney Rock in late March, that time she came after me with a pitchfork. My toes still hurt."

She folded her hands in her lap. "William worked all winter on that contraption. The girls and I did the chores while he hid in the barn behind a tarp."

"An inventor must have privacy. I was not about to let anyone steal my idea."

"Even your own daughters?" the judge questioned.

"A man never knows who he can really trust."

The judge frowned. "Please continue, Mrs. Westclock."

"It was time for spring plowing and planting. I determined not to do it all by myself again."

"How long have you done the spring work?"

"Ten years."

"How many years have you been married?"

"Ten years, Your Honor."

"I told her I'd help next year…that is, if we weren't richer than ol' man Carnegie and livin' on Nob Hill. I told you and the girls that, didn't I, Priscilla?"

She gave him a soft smile, "Yes, you did, Will. It was March twenty-third, early afternoon, I was about to shoe the mules when he announced his intentions to leave the next morning to demonstrate his…his—"

"Abomination?" the judge offered.

Her reply accompanied a coy smile. "No, that was a different machine."

"That one was a Gyro-Spudburrow, a self-powered utility drilling device," Mr. Westclock insisted. "It drilled our water well without any manpower."

"It did efficient drilling," Priscilla Westclock concurred, "provided the girls and I fed and shoveled up after the mules. But the wind blew down the tower. It did last longer than the automatic clothes dryer. That was last seen with a full load of wash, blowing towards Kansas." Mrs. Westclock dusted the railing with her fingers. "The wind whipped sparks from it into the wheat and we lost seventeen acres before I could plow a fire break."

"I've always been an inventor," Mr. Westclock said.

The judge studied her narrow, suntanned face. "You knew he was this way when you married him?"

"No, Your Honor. I didn't know I married him."

The judge gazed at the row of silent children. "You didn't know?"

"I thought I married his brother, Weldon. They are identical twins. Weldon and I were engaged for two years and even made plans for the wedding service. The twins set off to make a fortune in the Idaho mines. Weldon came back alone, and said William had died in a cabin that winter. After a time of grieving, we proceeded to get married."

"William passed as his brother? That would have been cause for annulment," the judge declared. "How did you discover the deception?"

"When our first child was born I wanted to name her Weldina, and he said, 'why name her after my brother?'"

"And you didn't run him off then?"

She spoke with firmness. "Of course not. I learned that Weldon hadn't died. He just found someone else more exciting. He wasn't going to even let me know, but William insisted on returning. He said it wasn't right to abandon a godly woman. He married me to make up for the less than honorable actions of his brother." Her voice trailed lower. "And I will always love him for that."

"So what happened back in March?" the judge pressed.

"William caught a breeze the next morning and was out of sight when I went out for the chores. I was mad, so I saddled a mule and went after him."

"With a pitchfork?"

"It was handy."

"She chased me around Chimney Rock," William Westclock declared.

"You in your Land-Darter, and she on the mule with a pitchfork?"

"Yes, sir. It was a frightening sight."

The judge turned to Mrs. Westclock. "You stabbed him in the foot with the pitchfork to stop him?"

"I missed what I was aiming at. I hoped to hit the gears."

"She clobbered them with a splitting mall when we got home. Took me two months to rebuild," Mr. Westclock said.

"I presume you were too busy to help with spring work?" the judge quizzed. "Yep."

"You rebuilt the land-darter and were ready to take off on June eleventh?"

"It was on June tenth, Your Honor," she corrected. "It's our wedding anniversary."

"He was leaving on your anniversary?"

"I told her I'd be back by Thanksgiving. Sooner, if I could get the financing arranged for building more land darters. Say, Your Honor, a small capital outlay of $1,000 would put you in line to double your investment within a year."

"Are you soliciting me?"

Mr. Westclock twirled his hat. "No sir, just concerned that judges' salaries don't provide the financial security a man of your stature deserves."

The judge brushed back his gray bangs. "Mrs. Westclock, please explain what happened on June tenth."

"I baked William a cake and gave him a present."

"For your anniversary?"

"Yes."

"They were too little," Mr. Westclock blustered. "She made me a pair of mittens that was way too small."

"They were tiny and blue, Your Honor," she said.

"If my wife gave me mittens like that, Westclock, I would assume she was announcing the coming of another child."

She dropped her chin to her chest. "This time it's a boy. He will be born on Christmas Eve."

"A boy?" William Westclock hollered.

The judge leaned his chin on his palm. "Tell me, without being too indelicate, how do you know it's a boy?"

"The Lord told me. I read in the book of the Revelation, 'He that overcomes shall inherit all things, and I will be his God and he shall be my son.'"

"I didn't know she was great with child," Mr. Westclock mumbled.

"What happened after you took Mr. Westclock the anniversary cake and baby mittens?" the judge prompted.

"He said, 'This is the opportunity of my life, Priscilla. I can't let it slip away.'" Westclock grabbed the sheriff's shoulder. "I'm going to have me a boy."

"And he didn't take the hint about the mittens?"

"William is a very smart man, Your Honor. But sometimes his mind is preoccupied."

"So, what did you reply?"

"I said, 'Get out of that contraption, William, or I'll shoot.'"

Mr. Westclock peered out the courthouse window. "I think I'll name him William Wadsworth Westclock, Junior."

"Willie Jane handed me the shotgun," Mrs. Westclock continued. "All the girls were there. They wanted me to shoot him."

"Why is that?" the judge pressed.

"After the gold converter failed, he said 'Shoot me if I ever want to leave again.' Then after the mechanical buggy wash scalded those horses in Cheyenne, he came back and said 'Shoot me if I ever want to leave again.' Then there was the potato powered trolley, the catapult mailing machine, the rollaway gallows."

"And each time he told you to shoot him if he ever wanted to leave again?" the judge asked.

"Yes."

Mr. Westclock strolled in front of the eight green-ginghamed children. "You know, if my boy turns out half as good as his sisters, he will be a wonderful lad."

Judge Young turned back to Mrs. Westclock. "And your daughters insisted on your shooting him?"

Wilma raised her hand and called out, "The Bible says we are to obey our parents."

"So you shot him?"

"I threatened to shoot him," Priscilla Westclock said.

"He wasn't scared?"

"No, he just smirked and taunted me."

The judge's gray eyebrows arched. "Taunted you?"

"Yes."

"What did he do?"

"I'd rather not say."

"This is crucial in this inquiry, Mrs. Westclock. What did your husband do to taunt you?"

"Please, Your Honor, I'd rather not say."

Wenetta raised her hand. "I'll tell! Daddy said, 'If you are goin' to shoot me, go right ahead. I'll give you a target you can't miss.' Then he turned around and waved his..."

"Wanetta!" Mrs. Westclock scolded.

"Waved his what?" the judge said.

"His fanny," Westalia giggled. "Then Mamma shot him."

"We all clapped," Wynonna declared.

"But Mamma cried, loaded him in the wagon, and drove us to see the lady doctor in Gering," Wendolyn added.

The judge turned to the lawman. "What is the report from the doctor?"

"He won't sit comfortable until after the first of the year."

Mrs. Westclock rocked back and forth in the hard oak chair and hummed a soft tune.

"Mr. Westclock, are you charging your wife with attempted murder?"

"No, sir. I just want you to lock her up for a couple weeks while I rebuild the Land-Darter to be operated by a man standing up."

"Are you prepared to go home and take care of those eight daughters by yourself?"

"Willie Jane can take care of the baby. The others pretty much look after each other."

The judge shook his head at Mrs. Westclock. "Madam, I have never met a more irresponsible man in the entire state of Nebraska. I cannot understand why you have stuck it out with him this long."

She murmured something so soft the judge leaned over the bench again. "What did you say?"

"You don't understand because you have never been woke up in the middle of a cold, dark winter night with a soft voice saying, 'Priscilla, darlin', I need you to hold me tight and rock me back to sleep.'"

"Is that enough to make a satisfying relationship?"

"It is for me, Your Honor. I have eight wonderful daughters and carry my son. Yes, soft words in the night are enough for me."

"She loves me, Judge," Westclock boasted.

"Do you love her?"

"She knows the answer to that."

"Perhaps she does, but I don't. Answer the question, Mr. Westclock. Do you love your wife?"

"I've always loved her." He dropped his chin to his chest. "Even when she was engaged to Weldon, I loved her."

"What are we goin' to do, Judge?" the sheriff demanded.

"This hearing is postponed until January second. Mrs. Westclock, during that time you are forbidden to threaten your husband with a gun, knife, pitchfork, hot poker or any other weapon, is that understood?"

"Yes, Your Honor."

"Mr. Westclock, you are to assist in the harvest and are not allowed beyond your farm unless accompanied by your wife. If you violate that ruling, you will sit in our hard cell until January. Do you understand?"

"January?"

"I would think you would want to be around to help name your son. You don't want him called Weldon, do you?"

"She wouldn't do that. Would you, Priscilla?"

She rocked back and forth and hummed a soft tune.

The judged slammed his gavel down on the bench.

Mrs. Westclock pulled on her green gingham bonnet and tied it under her chin. "What shall I do now?"

"Go home and pray that the wind does not blow and the buckshot heals slowly."

So that's exactly what she did.

*   *   *

STEPHEN BLY has authored over ninety-five books and hundreds of articles. His novel *The Long Trail Home* (Broadman & Holman) won the 2002 Christy Award for excellence in Christian fiction. Three other books were Christy Award finalists. He speaks across the U.S. and Canada, is the pastor of the Community Church, and serves as mayor of Winchester, Idaho (pop. 306). He and his wife, Janet (who is also a writer), live in the mountains of north-central Idaho in the pine trees, next to a lake on the Nez Perce Indian Reservation. Recent titles include *Paperback Writer* and *Memories of a Dirt Road Town*, both by Broadman & Holman Publishers and can be seen on their website: www.blybooks.com.

The Rhythm of the Current

Janet Chester Bly

The wind was picking up. Essie Makgill could hear the ruffle of the *Purple Thistle's* heavy canvas, the slap of rope against the spar as the ship rose and fell beneath her. A fine day for hunting whales. It had been calm as a ticking clock for too long.

Captain Thomm Makgill shouted, "Slip the anchor."

The whaling ship turned to clear the growing ice floes and aimed south to Baffin Bay. Essie pulled out her leather covered writing case.

October 3, 1859

> *Wind. God's breath across the water. But it's hard to write up here on the deck. The breeze yanks the pages. Other times, the capricious gusts tease us and determine what we will do from hour to hour. The moving air whips our faces in a thousand different ways. We trust our fate to the fickle whales and wind and our vessel's only half full of oil. Yet how I long for Scotland's shores!*
>
> *One more whale, the captain says, and we'll head for Dundee, full ship or not. Otherwise, we'll share another winter staring at bare walls at Baffin Island and another season on this smelly wooden prison. How I pray for a whale sighting.*

Just that morning an ocean-watching crewman fell over the spar.

"His fat eye and split lip are all we've got to show for our trouble," the second mate snarled, then kicked the clumsy sailor.

Captain Makgill barked a warning met with hostile silence.

> *I recall the young, earnest faces when we sailed the River Tay, the crew ready at their stations. They seemed so eager to impress their captain...and his lady. I'm officially on the list as assistant navigator, a post I'm proud to take. But*

now we are as tired of one another's company as we are the gray water, slate sky, and our wretched meals. And who can blame us? The long, weary months turned to years and our hope for sailing to Dundee with a full catch has ebbed. We hardly speak to one another, except for Mr. Grindle, the First Mate. He is a blessing on this bitter barge.

I'm working on a cheery face when the crew bumps against my bruises. I think my smile's a permanent crack. It's a wonder a woman can be shut up with thirty rough men for nearly three years and not go crazy. We talk of nothing but wind and whales. And I have learned the sad fact that I'm not near the Christian I thought I was when I boarded this ship.

The captain brushed passed her in his worn Wellington boots and dried, cracked oilskin coat. "Ye'll be havin' your island roof soon, wifie."

"Not if you get your whale."

"There's been no whales in months and winter's comin'."

They heard the cry of "Sail-O!" from the lookout.

Essie jumped up from her chair and gazed across the monotonous expanse. Crewmen rushed up from the galley. A bitter cold salt spray stung their eyes as they peered at a slight bob that inched out of the waters, weaving through the floes.

Captain Makgill trained his long glass on the faraway vessel. "Yankees. Looks like the *Imbroglio*."

The sails of another ship can look like the flap of angel wings. What a further joy to discover there's a woman on board. Talking to another female is almost worth trading for an ocean of whales.

Before they could speak and gam the approaching ship, "Thar blows!" rang from the masthead.

Essie backed against their cabin door as the crew scrambled into confusion to grapple with the tangle of ropes and boats. A large bowhead surfaced and blew mist halfway between the *Purple Thistle* and *Imbroglio*. The beast rested, taking in air. The full crew, including the captain, flung boats into the briny waves. The sight of that one whale invigorated them all.

The huge creature rose, arched his back, and began a long, slow dive. Essie tried to guess where he would surface. The oaring men spoke in near whispers, as though not to disturb a sacred ceremony, this dance of one of the great seafolk.

I hoist flags or shake bits of rag for the boatmen when whales are around. Such a splash when a whale breaches his body. What a show! But he is in danger. He does not know how much we need him to make our living, to provide oil for the Dundee jute factories.

The waters dipped near one of the Yankee boats. The black giant rose high, out and over, blowing, snorting. Its twin blowholes opened. A double spray of thick white mist soaked the crew. Its tail fanned out and the boat swung away. The enormous flukes smashed down, scarcely missing the bow. A wave of water almost sank them.

Captain Makgill stood in the bow of the lead Scottish boat, within striking distance, but the wind favored Mr. Grindle's vessel. He hauled his sail closer. The huge monster could just as easy bite any of them into kindling. The great fish headed toward a floe of ice instead and dove under. Three Scottish, three Yankee boats circled the ice to try to lance him out.

"That's our whale. We've been chasing him for days. He's got our flag," a Yankee yelled.

"That whale had no flag," Captain Makgill hollered back.

"If not, he's anyone's game." The Yankee lunged a harpoon under the ice.

Essie spied a shadow in the open sea. She waved a flag signal to her husband, but he was intent on the cornered whale. He poised his lance and got fastened, then lost him.

The whale burst through the water and rose between a Yankee and Scottish boat. In a quick rebound, Mr. Grindle's boat positioned right over the whale's back, where the head joins the body. The boatsteerer drove his harpoon into the whale's flank as Mr. Grindle shot a waif flag to mark it. But the huge fish got going again. They let go the gunnel and tried to avoid the deadly rush of rope. The boat lunged sideways, the hemp line running out too fast. Mr. Grindle snubbed the rope around the tongue post to try and slow it. The bow lurched downward. The boat's stern rose in the air. They let out more line as the huge fish sped away. With great reluctance, they cut the line to save their own lives.

The crew returned with long faces, but not the captain. "We'll come hame wi' a ship that's fu' o' oil, my lads. Let us do or dee!" he sang at the top of his voice.

One by one the crew joined in, then Essie, until the lookout shouted, "Sail-O!"

They watched the Yankee ship sail away through the floes toward the Davis Strait.

Mr. Grindle slapped his knee. "They're after that whale."

"And so are we," howled the captain.

"I saw shadows in the open sea—toward Dundee," Essie told him. "There's lots more whales that way."

"Wifie, one wounded whale in a bay comes easier. Besides, you'd see angels in the water if you thought we'd go back home," he howled with glee.

Essie braced against the rain and wind and gazed at the puffs of water dips pushing away from the ship. A dark speck showed through the thick mists. By late evening they trailed close to the Yankee ship. The wind whipped up showers and darkness covered the entrance to the bay. Essie took refuge in their tiny cabin.

About midnight they heard a gale. The vessel rocked and creaked. Boxes rolled about. Cans and bottles rattled. Essie was thrown from the swinging bed and feared they would sink. Each surge threatened to splinter the ship. She heard the captain shouting orders. Later, when the gusts changed from mind numbing screams to a soft whistle, Essie dreamed of a sea monster who tried to come through a window to pull her out and down into the depths of the waters. Whale shadows moved and moaned all around her with foamy gray faces.

> *I am not brave. I am full of little cowardices and foolish fears. The morning I bid farewell to Dundee to fix my fortunes with this ship and its captain, I was full of excitement, though I knew the risks. The three Balgreen brothers left by ship and were never heard from again by any of their wives. I determined upon such stories to share my husband's adventures, for good or ill. And we've had some ill. Our own cabin boy was swept overboard by a huge wave. We became quite attached. Only one convert and him lost to sea. The icy Arctic makes a cold grave.*
>
> *The ship's owner resented my coming because the captain may take fewer risks or I may get in the way of the hunt, or use up too much of the provisions. But some days I'm not sure I'll survive or I'm too sick to eat. I comfort my anxieties with the best service I can to my captain. And now I feel the flutter in my belly.*

By morning they faced both a snow and hail squall. But it eased by early afternoon. The crew studied the Baffin Bay waters and kept a close eye on the Yankee ship that stayed anchored. A good strong wind, a heavy sea, but the ships held steady. Then the *Imbroglio* whaleboats hit the water. The Scottish boats followed suit as a long moving hump grazed the surface.

The Yankee boats hurled out harpoons. The wounded whale rolled over and over in its death throes, thrashing close to the hunters. An artery flow sprayed into the air, painting the Yankees solid red. Scottish and Yankee alike sat watching quietly, like worshipers in church. The Scottish boats oared to the dead whale.

"He belongs to us," Captain Makgill screamed. "That's our flag."

Everyone knew this huge beast would boil nearly two hundred barrels of oil. The stakes were high.

"Our harpoons stuck first, days ago," the Yankee captain countered.

"But where's ye flag? It's our whale, unless ye can prove it's not."

The three Scottish whaleboats thrust their prows tight against the carcass. The oarsmen rubbed their hands along the bowhead's soft, rubbery skin. The Yankees cursed and scowled and drifted back toward their ship. Essie watched a woman on the *Imbroglio* deck, thinner and taller and bent over the rail. She longed to wave, to make contact with one of her kind, but knew this wasn't the right time. The men must resolve their duel.

The *Purple Thistle* crew tied the beast alongside the ship, began cutting in and fired up the tryworks for boiling the blubber. The Yankee ship head for the Baffin shores and the crude community of shacks that served as dwellings for the gathering of wintered-in whaling crews. Essie shivered from more than the Arctic wind. Soon she would be going home. The rhythm of the current, the melody of the breeze played across her spirit, a kind of dance she didn't want to end.

Heaven is in part being safe, still, dry. I shall also soon be free from the most noxious smells, a dirty vessel, bad water, hundreds of roaches…the long, gray miles left behind. I cannot wait to walk on a surface longer than the length of this deck. I shall not miss hearing the movement of rats at night in the depths of the hold. Only a short time left to endure bitter oatmeal, hard, wormy bread, and beef that tastes like old leather and burnt bones. I can purchase clean flour and do my own baking in my own kitchen, without a drunk steward's cross words. And not worry that the steward's fed us roasted rat instead of pork. But shall I ever be rid of the constant taste and smell of salt? I dream of sweet things—a tin of gingersnaps or Dundee cakes or even a bite of field tomato. But I do regret proving the cranky steward's prediction that I'll be a one-voyage petticoat whaler.

The captain let out a howl.

Essie sat up straight. "What's the matter?" she called.

Captain Makgill pulled up and over on the deck, a greasy waif flag in his hand. "Grindle found this buried in the whale's head."

Essie leaned forward as a wave of nausea hit her. "Whose is it?"

"The Yankees'."

The crew murmured and groaned. The second mate scowled. "It's too late for them. We got the whale."

"Oh, Thomm," was all Essie could say.

That night, as the crew cut and boiled, Essie dreamed of Dundee, of the day the wind blew hard and Thomm Makgill caught her hat and followed her to the jute factory.

"I'll return it, if you'll write to me every day," he said. "I'm leaving on a whaler tomorrow."

Essie refused.

"I'll write to you, then."

Essie received letters from every ship that sailed into port from the North Atlantic. When Thomm returned, she said she'd marry him "if you take me whaling when you become captain."

While he was still first mate, he hid notes in my gloves and stockings before he sailed, for me to find on those long, lonely nights. But now I see more of my husband and less of his heart. He wooed me better in letters from these seas than in being in the same ship.

The late night wind called to her, pulled her outside.

Essie got up and wrapped a blanket around her worn, wrinkled dress. She found the captain staring at the enormous bowhead while the crew worked. The deck stunk of whale parts. Her feet slipped as she slid across the greasy deck. The wind made ruffles of her hair. For the first time, Essie noticed how much each motion, each creak of timber, had become part of her. Hard as she tried, she couldn't recall the sounds of the streets in Dundee. She touched the arm of the man who made it so.

"You're right, of course," he said.

"But I didn't say anything."

"I know." He paused to touch her hair. Essie wondered how long it would be before she boasted soft curls instead of salt water and weather hardened stiffness again. "I shall give up the ocean and buy a farm in Dundee some day," he said.

"Perhaps. But until then, I shall try hard to make a home on this whaler. And I can paint and varnish the Baffin Island shack and make curtains for our bed there, too."

He nodded, patted her tummy, then tucked a note in her pocket. Before she could respond, he folded the waif flag in her hand. "I believe you need to visit a Yankee ship, to tell them to come get their whale. A lonely, homesick captain's wife waits your company."

So that's exactly what she did.

✷   ✷   ✷

JANET CHESTER BLY has authored and co-authored with her husband, Stephen, twenty eight books, including the Hidden West Series, the Carson City Chronicles, and *Hope Lives Here*, which can be found on their website: www.blybooks.com. She speaks on relationships and discovering your God-given tasks at women's retreats and family conferences.

The Delivery

Mindy Starns Clark

The wind was picking up. Leroy sat on a bench in Jackson Square, watching a swirl of leaves rise above the slate pavement at his feet. The few times Leroy had been to New Orleans, the weather was like this: dark, windy, heavy with the potential for rain. The roiling sky made him anxious and he clutched a canvas bag against his chest, feeling the sharp corners of the wooden box pressing against his skin.

Nearby, a group of children began playing tag around the base of a statue of Andrew Jackson on his horse. Leroy glanced at the kids in annoyance, not so much because the noise bothered him but because it seemed so disrespectful somehow, to be screaming "You're it! You're it!" in the center of a national landmark. Finally, he stood and walked out of the square and found another bench farther away, where the children's cries weren't so distracting. He had to concentrate. He had to think this through.

Inside his bag, next to the wooden box, was an address scribbled on a folded piece of paper. Leroy had come here by train, a fitting end to a long journey. Now that he was just a few blocks from the house where he would make the delivery and set things right, he closed his eyes and tried to calm his beating heart. After almost fifty years, he could still remember the moment he first saw the Stanfields.

Leroy had been folding back the sheets on the top bunk of berth 5C when he spotted them through the window. He had paused in his work to peer at the handsome couple for a moment and wonder if that was "Stanfield, Mr. and Mrs. George," who were taking the Sunset Express to Chicago. Quickly, he slid the bunk into place and latched it shut, then he hurried down the hall to greet them.

They were rich, he could tell that just by their clothes. The man sported a perfectly tailored navy suit, the woman a crisp skirt and jacket, her long hair held back by a headband.

"Mornin' ma'am, sir," Leroy said as the redcap handed up their bags. "Welcome aboard."

"Stanfield," the man said, his eyes never leaving the woman's.

"To the right," Leroy told them. "Three C."

He showed the couple to their berth and pointed out its features, though he was having trouble concentrating. There was something about the woman—not just her beauty but her posture, her attitude—that mesmerized him. She seemed so full of life, so nearly intoxicated with joy, that it was contagious. Her husband was certainly under her spell, as he gazed at her and didn't seem to listen to a word Leroy was saying.

Once he had finished, Leroy hovered there a moment longer than necessary, for some reason not wanting to leave. The man misunderstood the hesitation and handed him a five dollar tip.

"Sorry if we seem distracted," the man said with a wink as he started closing the door. "We're on our honeymoon and just a little impatient."

Leroy couldn't help but smile as he stepped back and pocketed the cash, marveling that anyone could be rich enough to toss out five dollar bills like candy.

He didn't see or hear from them again the rest of the day. That night, he spotted the woman in the nearly-empty club car, sitting beside the window. Leroy paused, wondering why she was staring out the window so intently when it was too dark to see anything but her own reflection. She was barefoot and wearing a white silk robe, her hair now loose about her face. It didn't seem possible, but she was even more beautiful than before.

"Ma'am?" he asked, pausing in front of the table. "Everything okay?"

She looked at him, and he realized that her eyes were red, as if she'd been crying. He wondered if the honeymoon wasn't going so well after all.

"What?" she asked, clearly disoriented, shaking her head.

"Can I get you somethin'?"

Her answer surprised him.

"Time," she said suddenly, raising her chin, defiant. "All the time I've wasted. All the time I've lost."

"We're fresh out of time," he replied, trying to make light of her odd response. "Maybe a drink instead?"

She didn't reply but merely looked at him. Had she been crying tears of joy? Despite her red eyes, that earlier excitement was still there, the nearly frantic joy that he found so compelling.

It wasn't that he was attracted to her, at least not in a man-woman way. It was something else. He looked at her the way one would look at a work of art, a fine sculpture, or a painting. No, he realized, he looked at her the way he might look at a movie actress, face enlarged on the screen, skin flawless and smooth, the image so utterly perfect it was hard to believe she existed in real life.

She reached for her purse, producing a silver case and, from that, a long cigarette. Remembering himself, Leroy took the lighter from his pocket and flicked it.

"What's your name?" she asked after exhaling the smoke.

"Leroy," he said. "Leroy Washington."

She sucked again on her cigarette, the red tip glowing in the dimness.

"Well, Leroy, you're still young, so let me give you some advice."

"Not so young," he replied. "Eighteen, ma'am." He figured her for her late twenties, so she had only about ten years on him at most.

"A babe," she whispered, smiling. "Married?"

"No, ma'am."

"Then listen to me, Leroy. You get one life. Only one. So make a wise choice, okay?"

"Choice?"

"About love. About marriage. *Wait for the right one.* If you do, the rest of your life will be your reward."

Before Leroy could respond, the door at the end of the club car slid open.

"Katherine?"

Mrs. Stanfield sat up straight and stubbed out her cigarette, the wildness suddenly returning to her eyes. She licked her lips, eager, like a cat.

"There you are," the man said, making his way toward her on the wobbly train. "I woke up and couldn't find you."

"Did you miss me?"

"Come back," he whispered, then he glanced at Leroy. "Pullman," he said, "a bottle of your best champagne."

Leroy felt a deep surge of emotion, knowing that he wanted what they had—a love so deep, so pure, that it was worth crying from the sheer thrill of it.

He brought them champagne in a silver bucket. As he gripped the cork-screw, he saw that the man was holding a rich wooden box toward his wife. She lifted the lid, revealing a pair of shiny silver goblets, their slender stems encrusted with sparkling jewels. She gasped.

"George! You didn't—"

"In for a penny, in for a pound," he said with a grin.

She pulled the goblets from the velvet-lined case. Then she held them toward Leroy as the cork popped free and the smell of champagne filled the berth.

"To my beautiful Katherine," the man said, holding up his glass. "May your beauty be as timeless as these goblets."

Before they could take a sip, the screeching began, the piercing shriek of metal wheels against a steel track. Leroy would later learn that the summer heat had caused the rail to buckle, but all he knew at the time was that something horrible was happening. The sound came first, then the sudden momentum of being thrust against the wall, the crashing, the screaming, the smoke.

Leroy awoke under rubble. Gasping for air, he thrust out his arms, pushing refuse from his face. Once he could see the night sky above, he stood, grateful that he wasn't seriously hurt. He heard murmuring and quickly dug through the rubble to expose the body of George Stanfield.

The man was breathing but semi-conscious, with low, dull moans escaping his lips. Leroy stood and looked frantically around, suddenly understanding that an entire portion of the train had been reduced to not much more than a heap of metal and wood.

"Help!"

He recognized the sharp whisper instantly. Heart pounding, Leroy dug Katherine Stanfield free, exposing her upper body. She wasn't cut anywhere that he could see, but her face was as white as a ghost and a small trickle of blood ran from the corner of her mouth.

"No," he said, lifting her and pushing the rubble away. "Not you."

"It hurts," she whispered.

He wanted to yell, but he could hear voices in the distance, other screams, other needs. Surely someone would come soon, to save them all. When he looked back down to reassure her, he saw it was already too late. He lifted her wrist and held it, but there was no pulse. Nearby, her husband was drawing up on all fours, conscious but confused, one eye swollen completely shut.

"I'm sorry sir," Leroy told him, heart pounding. "She's dead."

The man stared at him with one eye, processing, until he finally seemed to grasp the situation.

What the man did next had left Leroy haunted and confused for nearly fifty years. Leroy would've expected almost anything at that moment—crying, screaming, maybe pulling his wife's lifeless body into his arms and sobbing.

Instead, Mr. Stanfield simply stood up straight, looked around, and ran away.

Now Leroy was much older, retired from the railroad, and pursuing the mystery that had puzzled him all this time. Why had George Stanfield run away? Why did someone else from the family have to claim the body of his wife? Finally, why had he never attempted to recover the jeweled goblets Leroy had salvaged from the debris and hung onto all these years?

Leroy wasn't sure why he had kept them, but he felt like it had something to do with the woman who had died, with their conversation that night in the club car. It was like he had a responsibility to her.

After his retirement, Leroy decided, finally, to fulfill that responsibility. It took a lot of digging through old records, but he managed to track down an address. Now he stood and began walking toward the man's home. He rang the bell and told the fellow who answered that he had come to see George Stanfield.

"I need to return something that belongs to him," Leroy said. "Something from a long time ago."

"May I give it to him for you?"

"No, sir, I'd rather do this myself. It requires a bit of an explanation."

After a moment's hesitation, the man introduced himself as George Stanfield's older brother, Preston. He invited Leroy inside and then led him past ornate furnishings to a study at the back of the house, where a man was sitting at a desk.

"George? This gentleman has something that belongs to you. He asked to deliver it personally."

"Oh?"

Preston left and Leroy moved forward, thinking that even after all these years, George Stanfield's face was still vaguely familiar, a small telltale scar over his left eye.

"Sir, I know you don't remember me," Leroy said, "but I was your porter on the train to Chicago in 1958. I had just poured champagne for you and your beautiful wife when the train derailed."

Stanfield sucked in a sharp breath, half standing, his eyes darting toward the door.

"After I helped all the people I could, I went back and searched the rubble and found these," Leroy continued, reaching into his bag and pulling out the box. "I guess you could say I stole them, since I kept them for myself and never did turn them over to the police or anything."

"I—"

"I know it's been a lotta years," Leroy concluded as he set the box on the desk. "But it's been bothering me for a while. I thought it was the decent thing to do, to bring them back to their rightful owner, even after all this time. I'm sure they must be a family heirloom."

He cleared his throat and waited for the response. As he stood there in the strange silence, Leroy felt the weight of fifty years slipping from his shoulders. No matter what happened next, it was done. His errand was complete.

George seemed speechless, but before he uttered a word, his brother Preston stepped back into the room.

"It can't be," Preston whispered. Then he strode to the desk, pulled out a goblet, and examined it closely.

"I don't know what he's talking about!" George said to Preston, standing, panic evident on his face. He looked like he wanted to run away just as he had that night. Instead, after a moment, he simply collapsed into the chair, lowering his head into his hands.

"Tell me," Preston demanded of Leroy, "from the very beginning. How did you come to possess these goblets?"

He listened as Leroy described that entire day, from the moment the couple boarded the train until he held the scratched wooden box in his arms and climbed out of the rubble.

"After that," Leroy said, "I really did intend to find Mr. Stanfield and return the goblets. But you know how it is. I wasn't sure how to find him at first, and then a lot of time passed and I was afraid I'd get in trouble, maybe lose my job. That was wrong and I'm sorry."

"Don't be sorry," Preston said, his face an odd shade of red. "You see, sir, you stole something that had already been stolen."

Shocked, Leroy listened to the argument that ensued between the two men. Apparently, Katherine Stanfield hadn't been married to George at all; she had been married to his older brother Preston. Back then, everyone assumed that Katherine had sold the precious goblets, taken the cash, and run away—only to be tragically killed in a derailment. Now it turned out that *George* had been the one to take the goblets. He had stolen his brother's wife and the family heirlooms, thinking he could get away with both. After the accident, he had gone back home, feigned surprise at the news of his sister-in-law's death, and blamed his cuts and bruises on a barroom brawl in Biloxi. No one had ever been the wiser.

Leroy didn't know what would happen next. As the two men yelled at each other in the study, he retraced his steps through the house. Stunned, he thought about his own fifty years of misconception, his young notion about the "love" he had witnessed so long ago on the train. Leroy had stayed single his whole life, waiting to find that kind of love for himself.

Now he understood that what he thought was sweet and pure had been a lie.

Leroy opened the front door and stepped outside. The storm clouds had blown past, leaving the streets slick and shiny, and as he walked away from that house and its troubles, he felt the strong, sudden urge to get out of this city as quickly as he possibly could. The mystery was solved, even if he hated the answers he'd found.

An old-fashioned horse and buggy were waiting at the nearby light, and Leroy whistled. The driver leaned forward, an old man with a gold tooth and a top hat.

"Tour of the Quarter, sir?" he asked.

"How 'bout just a ride to the train station?"

The driver nodded, waving him aboard. Leroy climbed into the seat, took a deep breath and slowly let it out. He watched as the driver tapped the horse's rump with his stick.

"Giddayup," he said easily to his horse. "Get moving, girl."

So that's exactly what she did.

*   *   *

MINDY STARNS CLARK is the author of the Million Dollar Mysteries series, including *The Buck Stops Here*, and The Smart Chick Mysteries series, including *The Trouble with Tulip*. Mindy lives with her husband and two daughters near Valley Forge, PA. Visit her website at www.mindystarnsclark.com.

Fers Doré

DeAnna Julie Dodson

The wind was picking up. Alice pulled her ermine cloak more snugly around her slender shoulders and somehow felt the cold all the more. One last night. One last night of freedom.

She caressed the pampered kitten nestled on her velvet pillows, stroking it until her body relaxed again. It was not yet tomorrow.

Fers Doré was a beautiful city, prosperous, peaceful, the chief residence of Duke Édouard himself. From her marble balcony high in the Duke's palace, Alice could see the town rising from the placid sea, cobbled streets and snugly timbered houses and busy shops all centered around the glorious, heaven-reaching Cathedral of Fers Doré. Shuddering, she huddled more deeply into her cloak. A funeral and a wedding would take place in that cathedral tomorrow. The funeral of the old Duke and the wedding of the new Duke. Her wedding. Her funeral.

But she would have this marble palace to shelter her, ermine to warm her, countless attendants to serve her. What was there to dread in this? And, lest she forget, she would have the lovely Cathedral to delight her eyes anytime she chose to look down. Looking down on God Himself. Was there anything higher to which she might aspire?

Bon Dieu, she prayed silently, *if this marriage is not right, free me from it.*

"Lady Alice?"

She turned, startled, and then frowned to see a man standing half shadowed by the crimson velvet drapes. He wore a servant's livery and, around his neck, a heavy key. He was staring at her, a touch of pleased wonder in his dark eyes.

"How dare you come here, sirrah?" She narrowed her eyes. "You were not sent for."

"Alas, no, my lady, but I was sent." He stepped from the shadows and made a courtly bow. "To serve you."

Her sapphire eyes flashed. "I have no need of your service."

The man laughed, not unkindly, and again she narrowed her eyes, this time studying him more closely.

"You are an insolent rascal, I must say." Her taut mouth softened a little, into a snide smirk. "And in what have you deemed I am in need of help?"

He shrugged a little. "Leaving this place perhaps? Perhaps not attending Duke Édouard's wedding tomorrow?"

"Nonsense!" She felt a blush creep to her cheeks, hot in the frigid night. "Why should any woman refuse such honor as the Duke has bestowed upon me?"

"It is writ on you plain as day, lady, no matter your words. If I have read amiss, I most humbly beg your ladyship's pardon. But, if not, I can help you."

She took a step back from him, unsettled by his ability to read her face, her thoughts.

"Who are you?"

"I am called Will, my lady." Once again he bowed.

"Will," she mused, looking him over more closely.

He was comely, tall and well grown, and respectful enough, too, she supposed, but with a certain frank boldness that set him apart from the humble servants of her father's house. Will. William?

"Does not Duke Édouard have a brother called William?" she asked. "The one who renounced his claims to Fers Doré last spring in Édouard's favor?"

"Lord Roland William, lady, who should now be Duke Roland William." His dark eyes grew darker. "Lord Édouard has kept him these eight months locked away in the tower above you. Until he could make his claim secure by his alliance with your ladyship's father."

"Why was not Duke Averiel informed?"

"The old Duke had been ill those same eight months, lady, and hardly could tell night from day all that while. He had meant Lord Roland William to have Fers Doré and, if you will pardon my boldness, your fair self along with it. But alas, his heavenly Master had laid other plans for good Averiel and has since summoned him."

"But poor Roland William! To be so long imprisoned!"

"Why, lady, you sound as if you pity the man."

"So I do. Why should you think otherwise?"

"His cell is now empty, no thanks to Édouard. But I had thought imprisonment a light thing to you, seeing you come to it so willingly."

"A duke's palace is hardly a prison."

"Shackles, no matter how skillfully gilded, still bind."

Again his voice was cool and soft, and again she felt as if he could read her soul. Her sharp retort died before it reached her lips.

"What am I to do?"

"I can help you, lady."

She began to pace, pleadingly looking up at the vaulted ceiling ornamented with gold filigree. "I met the Duke but yesterday! Papa said Duke Averiel was a kind man and I thought sure his son would be the same. But he frightened me somehow when we finally met, and to know he's betrayed his brother—"

"I can help you, lady," Will repeated gently.

"But he will never let me go now." Her pacing grew faster along with her breath. "What could I say to him? 'I thank you most sincerely, Monsieur le Duc, but I should like to go home now'? Oh, bon Dieu, what am I to do? Papa has made the bargain. *I* have made the bargain! I have—"

"My lady!" He took her by the arms and forced her to look at him. "I can help you."

Remembering her prayer, knowing who he must surely be, she nodded quickly before her courage left her. "Tell me what to do."

"Everything just as I tell you."

She hesitated.

"Please, lady, you must do just as I say, or we will both be lost."

Again she nodded, and he smiled his reassurance.

"Everything is planned. We cannot fail so long as our resolve does not."

She managed a hint of a smile.

"Pardon my boldness, lady, but what are you wearing beneath your cloak?"

Color flamed to her face. "How dare—"

"I do not ask idly, my lady."

"My shift," she told him, seeing the urgency in his eyes.

"Get one of your maids' dresses, if you can, and some stout shoes and stockings. Now's no time for lace and silk."

She was gone but a moment. When she returned she was wearing a simple dress of russet linen. Her corn-silk hair was braided and tucked under a kerchief.

He led her to her chamber door and cautioned her to silence. "Follow my leading, your ladyship, and do not fear."

In the stillness of predawn, they had made it down the stairs and almost to the chapel when, hearing footsteps, he stopped. An instant later, one of the stable boys turned the corner and ran into them.

"What are you doing here?" Will demanded.

"I—"

"And why do you not bow before the Lady Alice?"

"Beg pardon, my lady." The boy bowed clumsily. "I was sent to seal up the old Duke's coffin before they take him to the cathedral. I'm to have it done before they come at sunrise."

"That must wait. Lady Alice wishes to pray for Duke Averiel's soul before they take him away."

She dabbed her eyes convincingly as Will led her into the chapel.

"Speak true, knave!" he demanded abruptly, looking the boy up and down. "What mischief have you in hand, coming here in the night? Duke Édouard shall hear of this!"

"Oh, no, by the mass, I've come just as I said, to seal up the coffin! Truly, I have!"

"And did you mean to seal it with no mallet to drive home the spikes?"

"Of course not. I have—" He looked down at his belt. "It was there but a moment ago!"

"Just as I thought!" Will grabbed him by the front of his leather jerkin, but Alice put her hand on his arm.

"You shall not frighten this poor boy so. No doubt he merely mislaid it. True, boy?"

The boy nodded gratefully. "I will go fetch it at once!"

"Her ladyship's prayers will likely be done soon," Will said. "See to the coffin the moment you return."

Once the boy had scurried away, Will grinned and held up the mallet he had filched, then he shut the chapel door.

"Now we must be quick, lady. Fortunately, Duke Averiel was a hearty eater."

He slid the lid off the large coffin and wrestled the old Duke's body out of it. "Rest in peace, good sir," Will panted, "and pardon this indignity."

Averiel was a very big man and, as Will had said, must have been a hearty eater. There was room enough for two—

"Oh, no," she breathed. "No, no, no."

Will looked at her from the other side of the altar where he had hidden the corpse. "Good thing the weather's been cold or they'd likely find the good Duke too soon for our liking."

She backed away from him, still shaking her head. "You can't mean—"

"I can, lady, and do." He took her by the arm. "Inside quickly and not a sound until we've been taken to the cathedral."

Surely a brief bit of fear was better than a lifetime of it and, this done, perhaps she would still have Fers Doré and, perhaps, a duke much more appealing than Édouard. Trembling, she got into the coffin and screwed her eyes shut. A few seconds later she felt Will crawl in beside her and drag the lid back over them.

"Not a whisper, my lady. We will be free. Keep your mind stayed on that."

As Will had predicted, the boy soon returned. She did her best not to shriek as he drove the nails into the coffin. Will's arm tightened reassuringly around her, and she felt the casket carried into the street and then up the grand stairs to the Cathedral of Fers Doré. The funeral would be later that morning and then the wedding. She would be missed before long. What then?

She relaxed against the warmth next to her. Somehow she couldn't help trusting this man who called himself Will, this man who risked his life for hers. She had been intended for him, for Roland William, all along anyway. And if, as true heir to Fers Doré, he someday came for his own, would it not be an honor to be his wife?

Before long the motion stopped. Will waited until there was absolute silence, then finally, thankfully, he pried open the coffin lid and freed them both. Then he took his pilfered mallet and sealed it up again.

"Now, my lady, this way."

He held out his hand for hers but as their fingers touched she heard the sound of soldiers' boots. The cathedral doors flew open, and Duke Édouard and a dozen of his men charged down the long aisle.

"Stop there!"

Before the Duke got more than a glimpse of them, Will pulled Alice behind the altar, then dragged her down the steps leading to the catacombs. Using the key that hung from his neck, he opened the iron gate, yanked her inside and then locked the gate behind them, imprisoning them in a terrifying darkness of death and decay. Why had she ever agreed to this madness?

"Well, well, so far and no farther, is it?" Édouard's voice was as smug and pompous as she remembered, but there was a sinister quality to it now. Perhaps because he knew there was no escape for them. "Did you think I would not notice my brother's cell was suddenly unoccupied? And, more so, that my dearest love was stolen from her chamber?"

Will pressed two fingers to her lips, warning her to silence.

"Do you think I will leave this place unguarded so you may steal away with what is mine, brother? Or do you mean to stay there until you are like those who are there already? Come out now or I will have the gate chained up and leave you to grow mad with hunger and thirst and the touch of the dead. Lady Alice, come now and you shall still be my bride."

Alice caught her breath but Will steadied her.

"As you please," Édouard said after a moment, and they heard the metallic clank of a chain. "I will return in a day or two to see if you've changed your minds...or lost them."

Soon the cathedral was again silent. Alice struggled out of Will's arms and rushed to the catacomb gates. Chained, as Édouard had promised.

"We must get out! I shall go mad!" She rattled the gates. "Let me out! Please, let me out!"

"Lady!" Will pried her hands from the bars. "You needn't fear, dear lady. We'll not be here even another hour. Follow me. There's a fresh passage dug at the back of the catacombs opening to a little cove where I have a boat waiting. We'll be away from Fers Doré and safe by nightfall, just as planned."

She laughed breathlessly. "Oh, I should have known your lordship would have taken care of everything."

"You mistake me, lady. I am merely a humble peasant, lord of nothing."

"You needn't pretend with me any longer, my lord. Even your brother—"

"If there is anything I have to be thankful for in not being a duke, it is that vile Édouard is *not* my brother."

"But—"

"My lady, Lord Roland William died last night. I carried out his plan for escape, but too late. Once their father was gone, Édouard poisoned his brother's food. You were first meant to be his bride and he wished, to his dying breath, to see you out of Édouard's grasp." There was a touch of malice in Will's smile. "I buried my master deep in the passage meant to free him. Édouard will forever wonder how his brother survived his poison and when he'll return to claim the dukedom. It should make for him some unquiet nights, I suspect."

"Then you are—"

"Not a duke, my lady, but still pleased to take you to freedom." There was entreaty in his eyes. "And care for you after."

She glanced back toward the gate. Through the bars lay the splendor of the Cathedral of Fers Doré and, beyond that, the marble castle due to Duke Édouard's lady. Will lifted one dark brow.

"You can go back, if you choose. Duke Édouard will love you no less than before, however much that may be. If a title and noble blood are what you require, they await you just beyond the gate." There was a touch of regret in his smile. "Odd how we cling to our shackles even after we've begged to be freed from them."

With a sob, she buried her head against his chest.

He turned her face up to his, looking tenderly into her tear-filled eyes. "I would sooner choose freedom and a true, loving heart."

So that's exactly what she did.

⋆   ⋆   ⋆

DEANNA JULIE DODSON is the author of *In Honor Bound*, *By Love Redeemed*, and *To Grace Surrendered*, a medieval trilogy, and is currently working on the Civil War novel *A Dinner of Herbs*. Born in Dallas, she graduated from the University of Texas at Dallas and is a life long Dallas area resident. Other than reading and writing, her passions are cross stitching; Dallas Stars hockey; her cats, Elliot, Emily and Eloise; and Psalm 47:6. Her web page is located at http://members.aol.com/missswrite/index.htm and she can be contacted at MisssWrite@aol.com.

The Deceiver

Doris Elaine Fell

The wind was picking up. I awakened to a gunmetal gray sky. Those fleecy clouds that hovered above me when I hiked to the mountain had drifted away. The clattering of bamboo stalks seemed threatening as they rubbed together in the gusting wind. September monsoon rains often crept in without warning, but even in my sleep deprived mind I knew this storm was different.

My eyes sought the top of Mt. Pinatubo, the sleeping giant. All day I had wanted to reach the summit and peer inside the volcano. Now steam rose from its crater. Red rimmed clouds hovered above it like a circle of fire. The ground beneath me rumbled and shook. The volcano, which had barely burped in a decade, hiccupped again, spewing smoke and ash.

My nerve endings went into high alert. Pushing myself to a sitting position, I groped for my backpack. Gone—and with it my trail food, passport, travelers checks, my watch. Everything stolen. As I stumbled to my feet, a young woman appeared around the bend in the trail, a camera and a flat briefcase in her hand. "Oh! I wasn't expecting to see anyone up here."

She had that right. All day long I'd hiked in the scorching sun from the base of Mt. Pinatubo up the north facing. There'd been a village off in the distance a few miles back, but I hadn't seen a soul. Short of reaching the top, I had hunkered down on the ground with my bedroll for a pillow.

The girl smiled. "I'm Emily Archer. You do speak English?"

I nodded. "Jayden Reynolds."

We were the same size, give an inch or two, and close to the same age. The girl was pale and wretchedly thin. Her eyes—blue like mine, her hair tawny and short. My face had blistered with a sunburn, hers was a pasty white.

"Come. We'd better get down the mountain, Emily."

"Just let me watch a few more minutes. I'm certain we still have time."

If she wanted to watch Mt. Pinatubo blow, I didn't. "I was just a kid when Mount St. Helens blew her gasket. I'd just as soon not watch another one this close up."

"But it caught your interest?"

"Yeah, as I watched the north face of the wall collapse I knew I wanted to spend my life following volcanoes."

"So that's what brought you to Luzon?"

I considered saying that the Philippine Airlines brought me, but refrained. I'd kicked around on my own for years, working my way through university studies. I spent my summers spreading myself thin—scraping every penny so I could study another sleeping giant. I'd seen some of the best: Mount St. Helens, Mt. Fuji, and Kilimanjaro in Africa. Popocatepetl in Mexico. Next year, if I lived long enough, I'd check out Mauna Loa in Hawaii.

Emily said, "The love of God brought me here as a literacy teacher. But I'm going home now and the first thing I'm going to do is attend a women's conference at the Cove."

I whistled. "Not a *religious* conference?"

"But it's so beautiful there. They have whitewater rafting—you'd like that."

Emily was right. Grudgingly I opened up. "My dad's a geologist. That's why I'm interested in the study of the earth, particularly volcanoes. Dad's been roaming around the world since I was born." Another gust of wind hid my tremor. "Whenever I hear of geologists at a volcanic site, I want to head there."

"In the hopes you'll run into your father?"

This girl hit the button. "Yeah. What about you, Emily?"

"It's God the Father who comforts me. He doesn't traipse off to faraway places." Emily's gaze roamed the mountain again, straight to the top. "I'm interested in the study of heaven. I guess you'd say I'm heaven bound."

Weird. She was definitely weird. When she faced me again, I saw the bloody rag in her hand. Her eyes looked dull, her cheeks sunken. A silver cross hung against her pale skin. "You okay, Emily?"

"Just another nose bleed. I shouldn't climb mountains."

A third rumble stirred the land beneath us. "It's an earthquake."

Did she think I was stupid? "Yeah, and I don't like it. There's an Ayta village maybe three miles from here."

She smiled. "I know. I've lived with them for the last three years as a teacher. They're a group of semi-nomads who depend on this land for their livelihood. But I'm going home soon." She patted her briefcase. "I have my plane ticket, but first I'm going to that conference in North Carolina. My mom's treat—I just came up to say goodbye to my mountain."

What kind of a whacko was she? Emily turned and watched another plume of smoke rise from its center. Mt. Pinatubo hiccupped again, louder this time, and a pale gray column blew into the sky.

"I hate to see her so unsettled. She's lain dormant for a decade. Never even a whimper out of her."

I grabbed Emily's hand. "Let's get down this mountain."

"I can't walk that far, Jayden."

It was a cinch I wasn't carrying her piggy back. "You got up here, didn't you?"

"I rode on the cart behind a carabao. Two Ayta boys brought me up."

"Then that's our way out. Where's the animal now?"

Emily glanced around. "Maybe the boys were afraid when the mountain rumbled."

"So am I."

We went a few yards with my urging. She touched my hand, her fingers as cold as an ice cube. "Maybe they will come back for me."

Behind us the smoke was black now, the smell of sulfur in the air. A mud flow was coursing down the mountain. Lava? If so, we were in for a cataclysmic eruption. I started to scream.

Emily yelled in my ear. "Jayden, there's the carabao."

It looked like a water buffalo to me, a massive dark critter with horns and a tail swishing back and forth. The Aytas used it to plow their fields, but we needed it to taxi us down the mountain. The animal stood in a rough harness, but I had no idea how to drive a carabao cart.

In desperation, I unhitched the animal and left the cart by the path. I loosened the rope that tethered the beast to a rock and boosted Emily on top. "Hang on to the horns."

"Can't. They're too far forward."

She reached out for her briefcase and camera. After slipping and sliding, I was finally sitting behind Emily, clinging to her with one hand and to the carabao's loose, thick hide with the other. We dug our heels into the massive belly and with a few prods got the creature moving down the mountain.

As the carabao lumbered through the muddy trail, she picked up speed. At the river she carved her own path, plowing knee deep in mud. The trunks of fallen trees, rocks and lava chased us down the mountain. Ash dust swirled through the air, coating our faces and arms. Angry screams erupted behind us and the animal lunged forward. We swayed, clinging to its flabby, loose skin.

I glanced back. "Two boys, Emily. Waving machetes."

"Thieves! Thieves!" they screamed.

The more they shouted at us, the faster the carabao plunged. I wondered if they had stolen my backpack. "If they catch us, they'd kill us just to get this four-legged monster back."

"Don't be angry at the boys, Jayden. Try to understand the people. The mountain is rumbling again. And they have depended on the rhythm on the mountain to plant and harvest their crops. If that muddy flow is lava, it will ruin their land."

Halfway down the mountain, Emily went limp against me. "What's wrong?"

"I have leukemia. But the mission plane is going to be at the airstrip waiting for me."

Emily was a missionary. I groaned and dug my heels deeper into the carabao's belly. The barefoot Ayta boys were still waving their machetes when we reached the village. The pilots were waiting on the airstrip. They lifted my new friend from the carabao. "We're taking you straight to the hospital in Manila, Emily. Doctor's orders."

She nodded and I could see how sick she was. What if she never got home again, never got to see the Cove?

Emily pressed her watch into my hand. "You lost yours. Take mine."

"I can't do that."

"I want you to have it. You see…I'm running out of time."

The pilot gave me a sympathetic once-over. "People are evacuating. We're picking up a nurse in another village. There won't be room—"

My stomach soured. They were going to leave me in the middle of an ash fallout with a mud slide racing down the mountain.

He gripped my shoulder. "You'll have to get out by carabao."

"I'm not getting on that thing again."

"They'll load possessions and people on carts. You can ride with them. They'll take you to the nearest town where you can catch a bus to Manila."

Emily was on board and the pilots revving the engine when I realized I still had Emily's briefcase. "Wait!"

But it was too late.

Three hours later I was on the bus—as far from modern as I could get. Pigs and chicken and roped bundles were stored on the roof. Someone had smashed the inside windows. No one minded the miserable conditions except me. I squirmed on the hard seat. My knee caps were pressed into the wooden bench in front of me. I balanced Emily's briefcase and my sleeping roll on my lap.

When I reached Manila, I called the hospital.

Emily Archer had hemorrhaged during the night and died. I looked down at her leather case and had no idea how to return it. I searched its contents. The plane ticket home. Her camera. Emily's passport. She wouldn't need them now. *Maybe if I cut my hair short I could bluff my way on board as Emily Archer.* I found the confirmation to the conference at the Cove, too.

Why not? I liked whitewater rafting. As Emily I would be guaranteed free room and board for four days.

When I reached Charlotte, North Carolina, I was beginning to like being somebody else. I was home free and headed up the Billy Graham Parkway en route to whitewater rafting.

Emily had called the Cove God's creation. I didn't know about that, but I felt like I had hit the jackpot. Fall had not quite faded away. We left the noise of the motorway and swept up a winding road through a wooded area alive with the vibrant reds and yellows of November. Fleecy clouds floated high above the Blue Ridge Mountains. I pictured gentle streams and a pristine river as I passed through the gate and checked in as Emily.

After I gave my name at the registration desk, the ladies behind the counter huddled in a flurry of conversation. Caught! I was about to lose out on my river ride and hang for deception.

They called an older woman to the desk. Her name tag said *Reagan*. Her eyes said sadness. When she spoke she was all charm and Southern hospitality. I saw tears in her eyes as she squeezed the registrar's shoulder. "It's okay. Welcome to the Cove, Miss Archer."

No need to choke up, lady.

I signed Emily's name and took the room key. "How early can I go rafting in the morning?"

Reagan turned back and smiled. "That's mostly for our younger campers in the summer, Miss Archer. This is a Bible conference. You'll find the conference schedule so full you'll forget about the river."

I didn't even own a Bible. I felt worse than I had when Mt. Pinatubo was spewing ash and rock. I'd used the last of Emily's cash taking a taxi from the Asheville Regional Airport. If I ran out now I'd have no place to stay. "Oh. I just thought—"

What had I thought? What was I getting into? No river rafting? And everyone toting a Bible?

Then they dropped another bombshell. "You'll be staying in the suite with four other women."

And me without a suitcase or change of clothing.

The next day there was a package of clothes at the door. Someone had good taste. Someone just about my size.

The meals were great. The women in my suite were nice. But in the conference session, a tall slender woman with Southern charm and a warm-hearted chuckle spoke about Jacob and Esau and the deception between them. They were strangers to me. I didn't care that Jacob had grasped Esau's heel at the birth canal. But what Jacob did kept me awake later that night. He had stolen his brother's birthright through deception—and his identity. The speaker called him *the deceiver*.

By the end of the third day, just before dinner, I folded up the clothes and put them on the bed with Emily's briefcase. I put her camera with the undeveloped film beside it, hoping that there would be a picture of Emily inside. At the bottom of my thank you note, I wrote, *I'm sorry. I, too, am a deceiver.*

I hurried down the long hall, past the pictures of Billy Graham, walked out the front door, and ran. As I ran from the wooded beauty, I heard footsteps behind me. I ran faster.

"Wait, Emily."

Catching my balance, I turned to see Reagan breathing hard. "I found your thank you note with my daughter's clothes."

"Then you know I'm not Emily Archer. I'm—I don't know who I am. But my real name is Jayden Reynolds."

"I've known all along that you weren't Emily. But why was it so important for you to come to the Cove?" She lifted my hand and fingered the watch band. "My husband and I gave our daughter a watch like that before she went away—inscribed to *Emily with love, Mom and Dad.*"

I was sweating bullets. "You're—you're Emily's mother."

"Yes. When she was diagnosed with leukemia, we tried to persuade her to come home at once. Will you go back up the mountain with me? I think you're one of the last persons who saw my daughter alive."

"Yes, ma'am."

"I want to know the truth. And I believe you want to know the Truth about Emily's God."

I glanced back. Dusk had not yet come. The remaining colors of fall covered the Blue Ridge Mountains. An afternoon mist was lifting. Sun filtered through the trees, putting a halo above the Chatlos Chapel. The spire rose to meet the mountain tops; its cross pierced the sky.

"I'm so ashamed, Mrs. Archer."

"Will you go back with me, Jayden?"

"Are you going to call the state troopers?"

"And what would I tell them—that you came here under false pretenses? That you used my daughter's name? I knew the moment you came that something was wrong. But I have to know why you were using Emily's name. Why you stole her passport."

"I didn't steal it. I kept it, but I didn't steal it. Emily talked about the Chatlos cross when we rode the water buffalo."

"It's a landmark for the lost, Jayden. Will you go back with me and finish out the conference? I'd like to talk to you about peace. About Jesus."

At last I nodded. "I'll go with you."

So that's exactly what she did.

*   *   *

DORIS ELAINE FELL's travels and interests are as diversified as her careers in nursing, writing, and as a missionary teacher in a bamboo schoolhouse. A Christy Award finalist, 2003 SPU Medallion Award winner, and recipient of a 2004 Silver Angel Award from Excellence in Media, she brings a sensitive pen, a tender heart, and a spirit of laughter to her writing. She takes you into a world of adventure—touching lives. Touching rebels. A teddy bear collector, not to mention an avid fan of the Tour de France, Fell is the author of twenty books, including *Betrayal in Paris* and *The Trumpet at Twisp* by Howard Publishing. She makes her home in southern California.

The Great Lobster Race

Linda Hall

The wind was picking up. Which would be a good thing if this was summer and warm and she was out on her sailboard.

But she wasn't. It was late fall, the wind was knife-like cold and she was heading out toward the open ocean in the passenger seat of Witching Hour, a very long and skinny and noisy cigarette boat with bullet holes in the hull. Driving this screaming monstrosity was Mr. Wonderful. Really and truly. That was his name. Well, maybe not his real name, but the name everybody called him and the only name by which she knew him.

When Dar needed to get where she needed to get to fast, and when where she needed to get was out on the water, they told her who she needed to take her there was Mr. Wonderful. He turned out to be a stump of a guy who wore an earring and sucked on a toothpick.

Sure, he'd be happy to take her out to pick up her lobsters. For a price, of course. When she'd tried to bargain, explaining about the deaf kids in Mexico, he'd merely put his hand up and said he needed to make a living. Clearly he was not interested in charity causes of any kind, unless, it seemed, the charity cause was him.

As they battered their way on the top of the waves, she realized that she had never been on a cigarette boat. And she'd been on plenty of boats in her short life and had more than a few sailing trophies to prove it.

"I don't like this wind," he was yelling across to her now.

Neither did she if it meant the boat would continue this horrific, mind-numbing pounding. That was the difference between this and sailing, she thought. In sailing, the goal is to be one with the elements; feel the waves and wind and work with them. Cigarette boating, apparently, was all about conquering nature, showing it who's boss. She held tight to a chrome hand grip.

"You sea sick?" He shifted the tooth pick.

She shook her head.

"I could put the trim tabs down, but then I'd get worse gas mileage. Have to charge you more."

Dar said, "I don't get seasick."

"Everyone gets seasick," then, "You some kind of Android you don't get seasick?"

She raised her eyebrows at that one. *Android?*

A few minutes later he yelled, "You know how many man hours are lost at sea because of seasickness on boats?"

"No."

"Believe me, it's a lot. All the ocean liners, the cruise ships, the navy. I have this idea for a movie. I thought it up because of seasickness. You get these androids. And they hire them to work on all the boats, you know, because they're not human and so they don't get seasick. They don't even have to *eat*, so you save money that way, too, Anyway—" he steered the boat until it was aiming directly to the sun. "The androids? They have a mutiny and take over the ships." He grinned. She caught a glimpse of gold tooth and suddenly felt like she was in the middle of a James Bond movie. It was after a ferocious wave knocked the nose of the boat nearly vertical that she noticed the series of tiny holes along the top of the hull.

"What are those?" She pointed.

"Those what?"

"Those little holes. In the hull there. They look like bullet holes."

"They are." He spat his toothpick overboard.

"How'd they get there? On the top like that?"

"How do you think? They were shot there. This boat," he said proudly, "among other things, was used to run drugs in the Gulf of Mexico. I got her off eBay."

She sat back and thought about that for a while. Then, "Do they interfere with the soundness of it? I mean, does water ever slosh in?"

"Nah. They're only flesh wounds." Miraculously, another toothpick appeared in the corner of his mouth.

Flesh wounds. She faced forward. The pounding continued. She slouched down in her seat. It was for the deaf kids, she kept telling herself. All of this was for the deaf kids. She checked her watch. Twenty minutes before she was supposed to be there.

The whole thing had started off as a bet. Well, not a bet.

"Let's not call it a bet," Mark had said. "Let's call it a friendly wager." They were a Christian group, after all. But, trust their young adults group to turn it into a competition. They were majorly competitive. You don't believe it, just wander down to the ball field every Monday and Wednesday in the summer. Competition was their middle name.

The challenge had been presented during their Bible study. A Mexican mission school for deaf children desperately needed four thousand dollars for a new roof.

That was a wad of cash for most of them who were students or just starting out. Still, they'd been presented with the challenge and decided to do something about it.

"We could have a bake sale." This came from Jennifer. They looked around. A bake sale? Who among them actually *baked*?

"Garage sale?" Andrea suggested. Which was a pretty funny idea when you thought about it, since most of them bought stuff at garage sales rather than sold stuff at them. Syl, who was writing their ideas on a piece of paper, suggested a car wash, but this was nixed by Melanie, who said that when the high school youth group did this, they only raised six hundred dollars.

"Besides, I don't want to get all wet," Melanie said. "You always get wet at those."

"How about a lobster boil?" Blair said. "An old fashioned lobster boil."

They looked at each other. The fall lobster season was due to open in a couple of weeks. And everybody liked lobsters. Hey, this might work.

An hour of brainstorming later, they'd turned the whole thing into a competition. They divided themselves into three teams, five people to a team. The dinner would be set for two weeks from Saturday, the day that lobster season opened. The three teams would assemble at the church for the nine A.M. starting gun. And the rules? As much as possible, the food had to be fresh. The lobsters would have to come straight from the sea, the eggs for the cornbread had to come from a farm, and the pumpkins for the pumpkin pie had to come from a field, not a can.

They would charge admission, but instead of people getting a whole lobster, like they do at your standard, boring lobster supper, they would take the lobster apart. The diners would get a lobster claw from one team, a tail from another, and another claw from the third team. Same with the cornbread and pumpkin pie; three small pieces of corn bread and three small slices of pumpkin. And then they were to mark their ballots for best cornbread, best pumpkin pie, and best lobster. The winning team would get a two-day kayak adventure tour in the Bay of Fundy. Scott, whose dad owned Fundy Kayak Adventure Tours, was sure he could work something out with his dad for a free package.

Dar's team had an advantage right off the bat. Her dad was a long line fisherman, so he knew some of the lobstermen who were now readying their boats for the beginning of the season. He called someone he knew named Bud Worsley on *Notta Nuff* who said if Dar got out to Herring Cove by ten, she could get a crate load of lobsters right off his boat. All she needed was a fast ride out there. That's when the harbormaster told her about Mr. Wonderful. Which is how she happened to be here.

Mr. Wonderful was going the wrong way.

Dar pointed. "It's over there. You're going the wrong way!"

"You want to stay out in the wind, be my guest," he yelled. "I'm going around the back side of Campobello. Where it's warmer. Okay, here's what I'm thinking. These androids? They end up taking over all the boats in the world, like the navy and aircraft carriers and even all the boats owned by private citizens. Like this one, even. Because they're sort of out of control and figure they own all the water."

Dar pointed. "Speaking of owning the waters, you're kind of close to American waters here." She began fishing in her backpack. "I'll get my driver's license."

He looked at her. "What do you need your driver's license for?"

"Picture ID. For customs." She dug out her wallet. "In case we get stopped."

He grunted and pushed on the throttle. "You don't know too much about me, do you? I don't normally pay a lot of attention to customs guys."

To their right was Eastport, Maine, ahead of them Lubec, Maine, and next to it the Franklin D. Roosevelt International Bridge, which spanned the narrow channel between Campobello Island in Canada and the mainland U.S.

"So anyway. There's like this one guy? I can't decide if it should be Tom Cruise or Steven Segal. And he knows the codes of the androids. Because he, like, saw them in an old painting. In a museum. No one else could decipher the codes but him. So he does and saves the world from the androids. So whaddya think?"

Dar blinked. They were headed for the Eastport public wharf. "Where you going?"

"See that guy? He has something for me. I just have to stop in for a minute and pick it up."

As they neared, a man in a puffy, gray ski jacket who looked just as seedy as Mr. Wonderful, gave a bit of a half-wave. Mr. W. expertly guided *Witching*

Hour to the side of the wharf and with one motion took the package from Puffy Jacket's outstretched hand. Dar could see it was a small something wrapped up in a plastic bag from Radio Shack. Mr. W. throttled down and sped away, but not before the guy on the dock said, "Hey! Wait! What about the money? What do I tell him about the money?"

Mr. W. gave a dismissive wave over the top of his head and they sped away.

Dar, still fuming, watched Puffy Jacket shake his fist at their departing boat and then walk up the path toward the road. She also watched as a police car drove down that same road. She also watched the officer stop the car, get out, and talk with Puffy Jacket. She also watched the way Puffy Jacket pointed directly at them.

Dar turned back and faced forward. "Who was that guy?" she asked.

Mr. Wonderful grunted. "Just someone I do business with on occasion."

Dar heard something behind them. "Yeah, well don't look now, but they're coming after us."

"That's not them," Mr. W. said without looking.

Then Dar saw who it really was—the U.S. Coast Guard. That's what they got for stopping in the U.S. without checking in with customs. "We're being chased," she said.

"Nobody chases *Witching Hour* and gets away with it."

Nobody runs from the U.S. Coast Guard and gets away with it either, she felt like saying.

The Franklin D. Roosevelt International Bridge lay ahead and they were heading for the narrow channel that ran underneath it.

"Do you know the current? Is it running in our favor?"

He looked at her. "That doesn't matter. Not in this boat. This is where we lose them."

"Don't you think you better stop?"

Once they were through the channel they would be firmly in American waters. In a Canadian cigarette boat with bullet holes and definite contraband on Mr. W's person. Which he obviously hadn't paid for.

I'm just picking up lobsters for a church supper, officer.

Sure you are.

She looked behind. The Coast Guard Boat was going through the channel, slowly, but it was on its way. She imagined the captain of that vessel radioing the marines, calling in the Android navy forces, the helicopters, the fighter jets.

Bullet holes in the top of the hull were suddenly beginning to make a lot more sense.

"Can you just let me off?" Dar asked.

"What here? Right in the middle here? You going to swim to shore? We're five minutes away from your lobsters."

The Coast Guard was gaining on them.

"Here's where we make our move."

He throttled to time warp speed and headed directly toward the island, then deeked into an outcropping of rocks. "Here's where we hide." He moved *Witching Hour* between rocks and turned the engine off. It was suddenly blissfully quiet.

"That's why these boats are so good," he whispered, patting the steering wheel. "They can get under bridges the cop boats can't. That's why they use them down in Florida."

"I need to be in Herring Cove," she said, checking her watch. "Five minutes ago."

"This is Herring Cove," he said. "We're in it now."

Dar looked around her. They were the only ones in this little field of calm and hidden water. *Notta Nuff* wasn't here.

Great. Just great. She dug in her backpack for her cell phone. Did she even have Bud Worsley's number? Somewhere it was on a scrap of paper. The boat rocked gently with her movement. She'd call her dad. Her dad could get in touch with the lobster guy.

"You want a sandwich?" Mr. W. asked. "I got sandwiches."

"No. I do not want a sandwich." She turned on her cell.

"Good luck with that," he said, pointing. "Won't be no reception out here."

She shook the phone. "So, what're we supposed to do?"

"We wait here until our friends have gone home. Then we try to find your little lobster boat." He leaned back and ate his sandwich, pulling his ball cap down over his eyes like he was settling in for a siesta. Next to them a seal raised its dog head and looked at them. Dar sat and waited.

Five minutes later, he started the engine and slowly they made their way out of the rock outcropping. The place was deserted, which Dar thought was strange. The U.S. Coast Guard didn't give up easily.

They headed slowly up the outside of the island staying close to the shore. "Tell me if you see your lobster boat," he said.

A moment after that, the Coast Guard boat tore out of another rock cropping inlet, heading straight toward them. They had obviously lain in wait, too.

"Please," she begged. "Can you stop this time? We're going to be in such big trouble with the Coast Guard. I've got a job and a boyfriend and I want to get married and have children. And I'd really like to do all this without a criminal record."

He turned to her. "The *what* guard?"

"The Coast…" she stopped. The boat moving toward them was not a Coast Guard boat. Same colors. "That's not the Coast Guard?"

Mr. W. leaned back and chuckled. "Him? He wishes he was. I owe a guy some money. For the GPS I just took possession of. He's obviously sent his goons after me." He took out the Radio Shack bag and pulled out a Garmin 426.

"You bought a GPS?"

He nodded.

The large boat which was not the Coast Guard was still coming toward them, however, and Mr. W. was still aiming away. Then Dar noticed something. The guy on the chase boat was holding something over the top of his head and waving it. It looked like—

"Hey!" Dar said. "That guy's got a lobster."

Mr. W. turned, raised his eyebrows and then shut off the engine. They sat there, lapping in the waves, until the *Notta Nuff* came alongside.

"You Dar McNabb?" yelled a guy in a plaid jacket.

"That's me."

"I'm Bud Worsley. I got something for you. Grab this line." Mr. W. did as he was told. "What's the big idea speeding away?" he added. "I got a crate load of lobsters for ya."

Mr. W. merely shrugged. "My passenger thought you were someone else."

Dar scrambled toward the side of the boat.

"Come here, Miss, take these off my hands. I gotta get back to work."

And that's exactly what she did.

*   *   *

Award winning author LINDA HALL enjoys a life filled with words and mystery—of the fictional sort, that is. A member of the Crime Writers of Canada, she is the author of ten novels including the best-selling *Margaret's Peace* and the acclaimed *Sadie's Song*. Her newest series of mysteries, *Steal Away* and *Chat Room*, features PI investigator Teri Blake-Addison, who's based in Maine and chases missing people—often finding much more than she expects. Her next mystery, *A Good Season for Whales*, is scheduled for release in 2005.

Linda has worked as a newspaper reporter and feature writer and teaches a popular course in writing fiction at the University of New Brunswick, Canada. She loves to hear from her readers. Visit her at http://writerhall.com

Garden Open Today

Veronica Heley

The wind was picking up, which was bad news for gardeners. Toni reflected that Aunt Gladys would not be pleased. Aunt Gladys expected the weather to be reasonably good for the Annual Flower Show and perfect for her garden's Open Day. Usually the weather obliged.

Toni wondered if it would rain. At times like these she regretted the sale of her car. But there you go. The car had begun to require a lot of garage time, and she hadn't really needed it after she'd moved back home to look after her father. What fun dear Daddy had had in his invalid buggy, whizzing up to the shops, and along to the luncheon club! He'd had a fine old time till that last stroke had put an end to his outings. Now he'd no more need of her, or of anybody and the buggy was up for sale, along with the house.

Toni told herself not to cry. Dear Daddy had lived life to the full and now it was her turn to live a bit. Soon she'd move back to the city and buy another car, something second-hand but reliable. She wondered if there might be a job going in her old firm. She must look forward, not back—once she'd got through one last duty weekend at her aunt's.

Aunt Gladys wasn't a real aunt, but a hectoring, ungracious cousin of Toni's long dead mother. It was Aunt Gladys who'd summoned Toni home when her father had his first stroke. Toni hadn't needed any persuading when she'd seen how much her father needed her, but she would have preferred to have made the decision for herself and not have been ordered to do it.

It was Aunt Gladys who'd arranged that Toni should apply for a job in the public library, which Aunt Gladys had run since the time of Noah's Ark. Nobody—especially not Toni, who needed the money—had dared point out that she was going to find it difficult to be chief caregiver for her father *and* put in the hours at the library.

Aunt Gladys had known the answer to that dilemma, of course. She'd graciously allowed Toni time off—unpaid—to look after her father, but she'd exacted a price for it. Toni found herself doing all the dirtiest jobs at work and whenever her father was in respite care or at the Day Centre, she was required to help her aunt in her garden.

Aunt Gladys was obsessed with her garden. Every year she entered a magnificent plant in the Flower Show, and was furious if she was awarded a silver instead of a gold medal. The following day she threw her own garden open, for charity. Or, as dear Daddy had put it, 'To play Lady Muck to her adoring public.'

Toni was expected to help with the last minute tidying up of the garden and serve teas to the public.

Toni paused outside the flower shop to inspect the plants for sale. Aunt Gladys always expected Toni to bring her a gift for her garden. What could she take her this time?

Would that double white pelargonium be suitable? Alas, no. It was past its best. Unfortunately none of the plants Toni was looking at were up to Aunt Gladys's standards. Leftovers, as you might say. Toni reflected, in a melancholy mood, that she herself was a bit of a leftover. Her contemporaries had married and produced children while Toni had been waiting for her long-term boyfriend to make up his mind whether to marry her or not. He hadn't, which was why she'd gone off to the city and made a new life for herself there.

She cringed at the thought of turning up to Aunt Gladys's without a gift. She could hear Aunt Gladys's voice in her head. 'Well, of course I don't expect gratitude for everything I've done for you, but I do think...etcetera!'

Toni was annoyed with herself. Why on earth had she agreed to come this time? She was worn out with the funeral, clearing out her father's things, and putting the big house up for sale.

'You're a wimp,' she told herself. 'Why not stand up for yourself?'

She turned away from the plants. Aunt Gladys always sent her to a local garden nursery to buy last-minute plants to fill the odd gap in her borders, especially if this wind was cruel enough to blow over an imperfectly staked herbaceous plant. Toni decided to get her aunt one of the new roses. Or that blue geranium which was so difficult to propagate but always drew admiring comments.

She shifted her heavy bag from one hand to the other as she walked down the tree-lined road. She'd brought three tins packed with homemade biscuits for the weekend. Aunt Gladys would pass them off as her own baking, of course. Toni sighed. She was not looking forward to telling her aunt that she was going to return to the city.

❦   ❦   ❦

Aunt Gladys's garden wouldn't have looked out of place on a *Britain in Bloom* calendar. At the front there was a prettily-patterned area of paving around a charming fountain, framed with unusual low-growing shrubs. There was, Toni thought as she unlatched the gate, a need for some colour. Undoubtedly Aunt Gladys would want to add some bedding plants to add spice to the well-planned arrangement.

'Oh, there you are! I expected you an hour ago. It's an absolute disaster and I don't know what I'm going to do about it. Where's your car?'

Toni kissed the proffered cheek. 'I sold it ages ago. I'm sure I told you.'

Aunt Gladys was grey. She looked grey all over, really, even when she was wearing black or beige. She made Toni feel overdressed in her blue denim skirt and pink top.

'Why did you sell it? You might have told me earlier.' Aunt Gladys was famous for not listening to what she didn't want to hear. She said, 'If only you'd come earlier, you could have got the cakes for me, but as it is I'll have to go for them tomorrow morning. I hope you've brought some of your biscuits for Sunday. I haven't had time to bake any this year.' She always said that.

Toni extricated the biscuit tins from her bag and put them on the table.

Aunt Gladys opened the tins one by one, and took one biscuit from each.

'I need a lot more bedding plants, of course. This wind! Half my taller geraniums have been smashed to the ground. You might have reminded me that you weren't bringing your car. That's the trouble with you young people; you just don't think!'

To her horror, Toni heard herself mumble an apology.

Aunt Gladys sniffed. 'You're looking peaky, but I suppose that's only to be expected. Sorry about your father, but he was way past his sell-by date, wasn't he?'

Toni wondered if Aunt Gladys had always been so unsympathetic. Perhaps she had, and Toni had got so used to being criticised that she hadn't noticed? She noticed now, all right. It reinforced her determination that this would be her last visit.

Over a cup of tea, Aunt Gladys outlined her plans. 'The herbacious plants will need staking again—this wind knocks them about something terrible. You can do that while I attend to the dead-heading of the roses. The first blush is over, of course, but the American Pillar is a picture.

'The big problem is my standard fuschia, the large one that I've been nursing all winter. I planned to put it in the Flower Show tomorrow, and then it would be the centrepiece for the rose garden on Open Day. But alas! It's been dropping buds all over the place and isn't fit to be seen. I've tried everything! I blame these cold winds we've been having.'

Toni murmured condolences.

Aunt Gladys sniffed again. 'When I was at the Chelsea Garden Show I saw another one, just what I needed. I had my money out ready to pay for it when this wretched woman said she'd put a deposit on it and wanted to take it away with her.

'Well, I wasn't standing for that. I told her it was essential that I have it, and I even offered a fiver more than she'd paid for it, but she wouldn't see sense. I followed her all the way to the tube station, trying to make her understand how important it was that I should have the plant, but she got on the train just ahead of me and...the doors closed on the plant!' Aunt Gladys was triumphant. 'She might have bought the plant, but it was so mangled it won't do her much good!'

❦   ❦   ❦

Toni found it soothing to work in the garden. She worked till dark, staking herbacious plants and tying back roses which had come away from their trellis. This wind! Aunt Gladys's back garden was long and narrow, but full of surprises in a series of differently planted 'rooms'. At this time of year, it was filled with roses of all descriptions. It was well worth the price of entry on Open Days.

'This is the list of plants that I need,' Aunt Gladys said at breakfast next morning. 'I would usually get them from the nurseries at the top of the road, but they were so rude when I returned a couple of things the other day, that I want you to go to the new place on the Common. I'll need my car to get some cakes that I've ordered from the bakery, so you can take the bus there and get a cab back.'

Who was to pay for the cab? Toni wondered, and knew that it would be her. She supposed she could afford it as she was her father's heir.

'You might look out for another standard fuschia for me, as well,' said Aunt Gladys. 'If I have it by noon, there'd still be time to put it in the Flower Show.'

Toni demurred. 'Don't exhibitors have to own the plants for six months before they put them in the Show?'

Aunt Gladys reddened. 'Well, I've had my own standard fuschia much longer than that, and I would have put it in if it had been all right and of course it would have won. So if I have to substitute something at the last minute, who's to know?'

I would, said Toni silently. She resolved not to look out for any such plant.

       ❦   ❦   ❦

The nurseries were difficult to find, being tucked away behind an avenue of semi-detached houses. But they were well-stocked. Toni was enchanted by the variety and number of fuschia plants for sale. Doubles and single, red and white and pink. Their bells danced. They were happy flowers, Toni thought. They made her smile.

There was one standard fuschia in particular, which was quite spectacular. It was as tall as Toni and almost as wide. The outer petals were a creamy white, but the bells were a deep crimson. There must be a thousand flowers on it!

The price tag was...ouch! No way could Aunt Gladys's budget stretch to include that fuschia, and it was far beyond the amount Toni had mentally set aside for a hostess present.

With a tiny sigh of regret, Toni put the plants she really needed onto a trolley and thrust it towards the checkout...to walk into a major row.

One of the check-out girls was accusing a belligerent, overweight mother, of refusing to pay for a bag of crisps supposedly taken by her red-faced, overweight son. The son was hysterical. Both women were threatening to call the police. The owner or manager of the nurseries was hastening to the scene, denim work trousers flapping.

Toni looked away, wishing herself elsewhere. However long was it going to take to get through the check-out now? Then she saw something which made her laugh. 'Excuse me,' she said. 'But I think you got the wrong person. Look!'

A half-grown puppy was in the next queue, being fed crisps by a tiny tot with large blue eyes and golden hair while her mother was absorbed in a magazine, waiting for her turn to be served.

'Ah,' said the manager, a nice-looking man in his forties. 'Did you take those crisps, little one?'

'Little one' was a practised charmer. She batted her eyelashes and lisped, 'Mommy said I could have some for Floppy, if I was good.'

'Mommy' came to herself, yanked the puppy towards her, and threw out a languid, 'I don't see what all the fuss is about. Of course I'll pay for the crisps.'

The manager met Toni's eye and they both smiled. 'Panic over.' The check-out girl relaxed.

The man said, 'I know you, don't I? Didn't we meet on a Gardens Tour some years ago? Can I help you with that trolley? That one's got a mind of its own, I'm afraid.' He had a nice face, a used, smiling sort of face. He was an outdoors sort of man, used to working with his hands. The nursery's success would be down to him, all right.

Toni smiled. 'I remember. We had a heated discussion about delphiniums; you preferred the pink shades and I thought delphiniums ought to be blue and not pink. Didn't you used to judge at Flower Shows?'

'Mm. Doing one at the weekend, come to think of it. Are you exhibiting?'

'Me? Oh, no. These are for a friend.'

An idea dropped into Toni's head. It was a sneaky idea. It was a beautiful idea. It was perfect.

She said, 'I was wondering about buying that fantastic standard fuschia you've got out back, but I haven't a car and I don't think it would go in a taxi, would it?'

Then she remembered something else, which made her turn pink. This man had asked her to go for a meal with him when the Gardens Tour was over, but she'd had to get back to see to her father. She'd been sorry about that at the time, but she'd forgotten all about him since.

He said, 'I'm afraid the van's out already doing deliveries, but can you hang around for a while? Get yourself a coffee in the conservatory, perhaps? I'll see if I can organise something.'

'The fuschia's so tall, I'd need something like the Popemobile!'

He laughed. He had good teeth and an infectious, crinkly smile. 'I was thinking of opening the sunshine roof of my old banger and dropping it into the front seat. Would that do?'

It would do magnificently. But, 'I don't want to put you to so much trouble.'

'I'm delighted. I hoped we'd meet again.'

She blushed and lowered her eyes. As if I were a teenager, she thought, embarrassed. But I do like him.

He steered her to the coffee bar. She ordered something, she hardly knew what. Her credit card would have to take the strain of buying the fuschia. It might be worth it, for all sorts of reasons, some of which she was hardly daring to let herself think about. He'd been a very new widower when they'd met.

That was one of the reasons she'd refused to meet him again, thinking he was looking for a relationship she would have been unable to give. Then. But now?

His car was an old Rover, with a capacious boot which took everything, except the standard fuschia. That went on the front seat, strapped in, with its glorious head sticking out of the sunshine roof.

'You're very kind,' she said, wondering if she were reading too much in his taking so much trouble for her. 'What do I owe you for delivery?'

'Supper on me. Tonight, after the Flower Show?'

She wanted to accept. How she wanted to! But, 'Forgive me, but I don't usually accept…oh, that sounds so…but you see, I'm not used to…well, I suppose you can see that.'

'Heartsease,' he said. 'Your eyes reminded me of pansies, the dark, velvety ones. I remember you looked after your father. Is he still…?'

'He died six weeks ago. At home. It was lovely that he could stay at home, but I'm selling up now. The house is too big for me, and I need to get away, make a fresh start.'

'You're not going to move far, are you? Not now I've found you again?'

He unloaded the car for her, and gave her his phone number, saying he'd call for her at eight that evening.

Now to see if Aunt Gladys would fall into the trap. If she didn't, then there was no harm done, and the fuschia would make a superb centrepiece in her garden when she opened it to the public. However, if she put it into the show, the judges—and one judge in particular—would know where it came from, and the word would go around that Aunt Gladys had cheated. It was entirely up to Aunt Gladys, thought Toni, as she humped plants up the path and rang the doorbell.

She waved goodbye to the nurseryman, thinking that if he really did want to see her again, perhaps she wouldn't bother to return to the city but find a flat to rent close by. And that perhaps, if all went well, one day he might propose their working on a garden together. She would demur at first, of course, but eventually accept.

So that's exactly what she did.

*   *   *

VERONICA HELEY has had fifty titles published so far, including crime, historical, and biography for adults. She has also written many books of fiction and resource materials with a Christian background for children of all ages.

She has contributed playlets for a telephone storyline, storyboards for cartoons, and book reviews and articles in the Christian press.

She is a long-time member of the Association of Christian Writers and served four years as their Events Organiser. She has taught in Junior Church, run a Youth Club, and devised and organised Holiday Clubs. She runs the bookstall at her church, and produces a monthly Reminder for Prayer. She is currently writing the Ellie Quicke Mysteries for Severn House—which takes Christian values out into the marketplace—and the Eden Hall series for Zondervan, a romance series set in a stately home in the Cotswolds.

Married to a probation officer, she has a grown-up musician daughter and lives in London.

Second Glance

Roxanne Henke

<u>Alessandra</u>

The wind was picking up. With a flick of my hand I brushed long strands of hair away from my eyes and hurried my steps. In this crowd it was an effort to keep focused. To keep my eyes on the man in the brown jacket. Could it really be *him*? I was determined to find out. Whoever it was, he side-stepped meandering tourists much better than I did.

Of course side-stepping was easier when you wore brown loafers and not ridiculously-high, designer heels. If I would have known I was going to spot him outside the Hotel Luna, I would have dressed differently. Maybe tennis shoes and a running suit instead of heels and a blue Armani dress. But then, what should a person wear to chase after the man who shattered a dream?

<u>Mark</u>

I glanced quickly over my shoulder. I felt like I was being followed, which was ridiculous. Who would be following me? A small-town businessman from the Midwest on a walking tour on the Isle of Capri, or 'CAW-pree' as our Italian tour guide pronounced it, wasn't exactly an object of international intrigue.

I let my wife-of-a-week, Sara, step in front of me as we followed our guide past the entrance of the famous five-star Hotel Luna. Fat chance Sara and I would ever be staying there. It wasn't so much I couldn't afford it, more that I didn't choose to spend my hard-earned money on fancy pillows in high-brow hotels. Our low-rent digs on the other side of Capri, in Annacapri, were just fine.

"Qweekly." The tour guide hurried our small group across the busy street towards the funicular, the tram-like train that would take us down to the souvenir shops near the beach.

As I reached the curb, I looked behind me, making sure all the people in our group had made it across. A flash of blue caught my eye. *Her?* Across the street in Capri? It couldn't be. A large group of tourists lumbered between us. If it was her—

I stared. Tried to glance between the bobbing bodies. Waited for them to pass. *Hurry!*

No, don't.

What would I do if it was her? Apologize? Ask for forgiveness? Or run away? Again.

Alessandra

I stepped one foot off the curb, quickly pulled back. It wouldn't accomplish much to get run over by a Vespa—or a dozen of them—before I had a chance to talk to him. Get his side of the story once and for all. I glanced at my watch. I had another half hour until my business meeting, time enough for him to explain why he'd left. Then again, he could talk for a lifetime and I wasn't sure I'd understand.

Where was he? I ducked my head, trying to peer between the traffic and the never-ending tourists. What if I'd lost him?

Would it matter? Maybe you're better off not knowing for sure. If he hadn't left you would have never—

Ah, *there* he was. His brown hair and navy jacket were moving away from me. If I was ever going to talk to him, now was the time.

If I could catch him.

Mark

"When the fu-nee-cular stops, enter qweekly." The tour guide herded our small group near the wall of the waiting area. "We won't all fit into one-a car, so keeepa an eye oh-pen and meeet together at the bottom of the heeel."

I shot Sara a look. "Heel?" I mouthed, pointing to my shoe.

She flashed me a grin, rose up on tiptoes. "Hill," she whispered into my ear. Her ear had attuned to our guide's accented-English better than mine.

I wrapped an arm around Sara's waist and pulled her close. This wasn't the first time I'd realized how lucky I was to have married her. What a mistake it would have been if I'd—Out of the corner of my eye I spotted a flash of familiar blue. There was that woman again. The one who looked so much like—

It couldn't possibly be *her*...could it? Had she waved? I turned to look beside me. Maybe an Italian friend of hers was in the cluster of people next to our group. Maybe she knew our guide. Or me.

For my own peace of mind, I needed to know if it was her. This wouldn't be much of a honeymoon for Sara or me if my mind was on another woman. Just as I turned my head, determined to get a good look, the funicular roared into the station. A crowd of people exited the train, quickly replaced in the small, ski-lift-like cars by another mass of people. Sara stood close in front of me. I shuffled forward, trying to move away from the rapidly closing doors. A quick jolt and we were heading down the hill. Automatically, I looked ahead to where we'd be going, then back, to see the spot where we'd been. My eyes locked on the woman in blue, standing behind the glass of the tram car directly behind ours. I looked away as a wash of relief flooded through me. It wasn't her.

Why would it be so awful if it was?

Well, because...My mind scrambled, trying to put those lost months into focus. Those months when I told Sara I wasn't ready for the relationship she wanted. When I told her I needed space and then did my best to prove to myself that no one...no one, could *make* me love them.

I remembered Sara's sobs. Then her quiet tears. Finally, her resigned words. "I love you, Mark. But I don't love you more than God does. When you find His love, then you might be ready for mine. I hope you find it someday." Then she got out of the car and walked away into the night.

What had it been? Almost a year of running? Of denying I needed anyone. I'd thought I was running from Sara...I'd learned I was running from myself. From demons that had led me to believe happiness could come from a hot-shot career. From pushing my own agenda and not caring about anyone else. Certainly not from the many beautiful women I pretended to be interested in...

"They're a diversion from work," I'd told myself.

Deep down, I knew I was doing my best to distance myself from my blue-collar family. I wasn't going to let some minimum-wage job dictate my life the way my dad had. I wasn't going to rely on faith and a prayer to put food on my table, living from paycheck to paycheck and taking handouts in-between. I remembered clearly the hot shame I felt when my high school basketball coach told me he'd find me a scholarship to go to freshman basketball camp. He knew as well as I that my family couldn't afford to send me. No, I'd determined way back then that my life was going to be different. I was going to *make something* of myself. I knew even then I couldn't count on Dad to help me. Or his God. I was going to have to do it all on my own.

And I had. Until the first time Sara said she loved me…and waited for me to love her back. It was too soon. I wasn't anywhere near the top of any ladder I hoped to climb. All I could see was the journey ahead. The one I'd planned to make alone.

Tell that to your heart.

I'd pushed those words away and Sara, too. Then followed a string of other women, all of whom I kept at arm's-length, not letting our relationships get to the point where the word "love" would be expected. Until…

I looked over my shoulder, through the glass, at the woman who stared back at me. It wasn't *her*, but it had been someone very much like her who pushed me back to Sara…back to God. A woman who had the same empty goals I did…to get to the top no matter who you had to step on to get there.

Before I had time to remember more, the strange train screeched to a stop and a mass of people pushed me onto the street.

Alessandra

The funicular was nearing the bottom of the slope. I would need to be quick in these expensive heels to get off the train and reach him before he disappeared into the mass of tourists that always crowded the beach below.

Suddenly my chest felt tight. What would I say? What should a woman say to the man who fathered her child…and then left? Before he knew if it was a boy or a girl. Without saying, "I'll be back." Or, as a consolation, "Maybe someday…"

What would I say?

No matter. I didn't have time to think about it. The words would come.

The train jolted to a stop and I maneuvered my way out the doors. There. There he was. I shouldered my way through the crowd. Three quick steps and I'd be near enough to touch him.

Two.

One.

I reached out my hand. "Giovanni?"

He turned. The man who had looked so much like *him* from across a busy street was a perplexed-looking tourist. A man who had the same dark hair as Gio, the same dark eyes and strong chin…but was not…*him*.

"I'm sorry. I—" My hand dropped. "You looked so much like—"

"Funny," he laughed, his broad, American accent sounding so foreign in such a familiar face, "you look like someone I used to know, too. Small world."

"Yes. Yes, it is." I turned away, suddenly realizing I didn't need to say anything. Even if it had been Gio, the words I thought I needed to say were gone. Along with the callused heart he'd left me with. His leaving had at first sent me reeling, then sent me to a Father who would never leave. Would I change that?

Of course not. Not a moment of it.

Mark

Sara watched the attractive woman walk away. "Who was that?"

I shook my head. "I don't know. She said I looked like someone she knew." A flash of quick memories flooded my brain. They left when Sara threaded her arm through mine and squeezed her shoulder tight against me.

"I hope it was someone who made her happy," Sara said.

"Yeah. Me, too." I looked down at Sara. Into her blue eyes. Love. That's all I saw. I was so lucky to have her.

Alessandra

I walked away, suddenly very glad it hadn't been Gio. There was nothing to say after all. My daughter was a blessing I wouldn't have without him. What I'd learned from that failed relationship had made me so much stronger...and humble.

I looked back, taking one more glimpse of the man who'd unknowingly shown me how good my life was. The woman at his side was looking up at him. He was looking down at her.

I found myself hoping beyond all hope that the woman beside him would stand on her tip toes and kiss him. For me. For all I had learned from a man who looked so much like him.

Kiss him. I thought. *Kiss him.*

For endings, and new beginnings, and all things in-between.

I saw her rise up on her toes.

Kiss him. Every nerve-ending in my being focused on her. *Kiss him!* As if my wishing and praying could make it so. *Kiss him!*

So that's exactly what she did.

*   *   *

ROXANNE HENKE is the author of *After Anne, Finding Ruth, Becoming Olivia*, and *Always Jan*, published by Harvest House Publishers. She is currently at work on the final book in the Coming Home to Brewster series. She lives in rural North Dakota with her husband, Lorren, and an annoyingly-friendly dog named Gunner. Roxanne and her husband have two young adult daughters who are also friendly, but not annoying!

You can find Roxy on the web at www.roxannehenke.com.

Beauty Queen

Angela Hunt

The wind was picking up.

Malena Osborne smiled and tried not to think about what the breeze was doing to her hair. She'd spent twenty minutes on it this morning, working with paste and mousse and spray to achieve an artfully unarranged look.

"Okay, ladies." The photographer's assistant held up her hand. "On three, give me an energized 'yeah.' One, two, three!"

"Yeah!" Lifting her brows, Malena did her best to inject a little extra sparkle into her grin. She'd already brushed a film of Vaseline over her teeth and her new lip gloss was supposed to stay in place at least four hours.

"Keep smiling, ladies!" Marcy Harcourt, the pageant coordinator, called encouragement from the sidelines. "Remember—only a few more hours until your big night!"

Malena froze her smile and turned toward another photographer, a bearded fellow with a press pass dangling from his neck. She and fifty-one other girls had been herded from photo op to photo op for the last three days. They'd toured the Vehicle Assembly Building at Cape Kennedy and posed in front of a space shuttle; they'd splashed in the surf on Cocoa Beach and pretended to fish from a pier. Now they were lined up in front of the original Ron Jon's Surf Shop, smiling like politicians.

Malena's cheeks ached from the stress of constant smiling. At moments like this she wanted to strangle the college friend who had signed her up for her first pageant, Miss Tangerine Bowl. "You're nice, pretty, and you like fruit," Joyce had told her when the preliminary acceptance letter arrived last year. "Go for it."

"But I don't want to be Miss Tangerine! I want to study!"

"The title comes with a five hundred dollar scholarship."

The thought of earning five hundred dollars away from the serving line of the college cafeteria proved irresistible, and Malena had been flabbergasted when she won the title. She had never been the frou-frou type and her God-given dream of working with the elderly wouldn't require any kind of fashion sense. But since her tuition bill would exceed forty thousand dollars by the time she graduated with a degree in geriatric medicine, she decided it might be wise to temporarily apply herself to the science of beauty.

Within a few months of winning that first pageant she'd gone on to win "Miss Strawberry Festival," "Miss Orange Blossom," and "Miss Tangelo Fair."

Along the way, she whittled her frame to a size six and made Pilates part of her daily routine. She haunted cosmetics counters and begged the salesgirls for makeup tricks. She splurged on "miracle" foundation garments at Victoria's Secret, trusting bits of fiberfill and wire to replace the curves she'd dieted away.

She read *Time* and *Newsweek* to stay up on current events; she studied fashion magazines from cover to cover. She signed up for a credit card and invested five thousand dollars in a better smile, all because she had her eye on the present prize—a thirty thousand dollar scholarship and the title of "Miss American Pride."

"Okay, girls." Miss Follow-the-Rules-or-Be-Disqualified Harcourt clapped for their attention. "If you'll move into the parking lot, Ritchie Nelson is waiting to explain our next project."

Feeling like a mindless speck in a perfumed paramecium, Malena turned away from the cameras and stepped to the left.

"You've got to be kidding." Miss Puerto Rico groaned as they walked. "They don't expect us to get into those things, do they?"

Malena followed her neighbor's gaze. In the parking area, another man with a press pass stood before a line of—

"Rickshaws?" Miss District of Columbia supplied the word. "What in the world are *rickshaws* doing in Cocoa Beach?"

Ritchie Nelson held up his hands for quiet. "Greetings, ladies," he said, grinning. "And thank you for coming out. In order to promote Ritchie's Rickshaw service, we're going to take a few photos with you lovely ladies in our vehicles. We'll do this one at a time, but we have several conveyances and promise to make this as painless as possible." He glanced at his list, then looked up. "We'll start with Miss Alabama. Misses Alaska, Arizona, and Arkansas, fall in behind her," Ritchie bellowed. "Step up to a buggy and climb on in."

Malena crossed her arms as the sea around her shifted. Miss Alabama, who'd settled into her rickshaw, nearly lost her colored contacts when a hunky, tanned young man stepped between the handles. "Ohmigoodness," she cooed, "*please* tell me you're taking me for a ride?"

"Cool your jets, Alabama," Ritchie called. "Victor is only a prop."

Malena felt embarrassed for poor Victor. The runner was young, probably about her age. He wore black shorts, white socks, running shoes, and a sleeveless tank top with "Ritchie's Rickshaws" emblazoned across the front. His dark hair rose above his head in short spikes—paste or pomade?—and his face, or what she could see of it, seemed strong. Unlike the guys at the other rickshaws, he wasn't drooling all over himself or walking around with his arms bent in an artificial flex.

What would make a young man take a sweaty job like this? Maybe, like her, he was trying to earn money for college.

"Misses California, Colorado, Connecticut, and Delaware," Ritchie called.

Malena carefully pushed a clump of hair out of her eyes. If this hairdo held up, she wouldn't have to shampoo again before tonight, which meant she might squeeze in a power nap this afternoon...

Cameras whirred; the second group of girls climbed out of the rickshaws. Ritchie glanced at his list. "Misses Florida, Georgia, Hawaii, and Idaho, please."

Pasting on a smile, Malena approached the first vehicle. Because Ritchie was busy helping Miss Georgia free her heel from a crack in the sidewalk, Malena walked to Victor's side. "Should I just get in?"

He blinked, then nodded as a flush crept up his neck.

Malena shook her head as she stepped over the handle and slid onto the padded vinyl seat. A lot of guys were shy around beauty queens, but Victor was the shyest she'd met.

She settled into the woven straw shell, grateful for a moment's shelter from the blazing sun.

Poor Victor didn't have any shade at all.

"Been doing this long?" she asked.

The young man hesitated, then glanced over his shoulder. "Um...uh huh."

"Do you enjoy it?"

He lifted the rig and assumed a runner's pose. "Yeah."

She was about to ask another question, but Ritchie and his photographer moved into position. "Okay, Miss Florida, let's see what you've got," Ritchie called. "Come on, pretty lady, how about showin' a little leg?"

She was about to give him a frosty smile when Victor took off, sprinting over an open stretch of asphalt with Malena and his rickshaw.

"Hey," the photographer called, "where'd she go?"

Bewildered, Malena clung to the side of the moving vehicle with one hand while she protected her hair with the other. "What are you *doing*?"

Victor didn't answer, but shifted into an easy lope and pulled into the bicycle lane.

Malena turned around. Through a rectangular vinyl window in the back of the buggy she could see a handful of people peering down the highway. One of them, Marcy Harcourt, waved frantically and pointed at the departing rickshaw.

Too stunned to speak, Malena stared at the back of Victor's head. What in the world had possessed this guy? Was he taking her around the block because he was mad at his boss, or was this some bizarre kidnapping plot?

"Hey, Victor." She managed a stilted laugh. "Why don't you take a right at this next corner so we can go back to Ron Jon's."

She waited, but Victor passed the corner without slowing. He continued southward, his shoes pounding the pavement at a steady clip.

"Okay, Vic." She struggled to remain calm. "We need to go back. Miss Idaho is waiting for you. Miss Illinois, too."

"We-have-to-go-somewhere-else." He panted the words, pronouncing each syllable in rhythm with his steps.

Malena looked at the highway to her left, waiting for the inevitable police car. Marcy would wait maybe five seconds before screaming for the cops. If Victor didn't turn this contraption around, she'd call the FHP, FBI, and CIA. She'd put a law enforcement alphabet soup on Victor's trail before she let anything sully her precious pageant.

Malena crossed her arms and stared at the back of Victor's head. The man might be crazy, but the line at the back of his neck was as straight as a ruler, his skin clean and tidy. Miss Texas said you could tell a lot about a guy by his hairline; a man who kept his neck clean generally kept his life clean, too.

If only Miss Texas were here now. Malena glanced to her right and saw clumps of tourists on the sidewalk; several waved at Malena as she whizzed by.

"Victor," she firmed her voice, "this has gone far enough. I've enjoyed the ride, but you're going to be in serious trouble if you don't turn around."

She waited. No response.

"Victor, I'm going to scream—see those people up ahead? I'm going to tell them to call the police."

"Don't worry." Victor kept his eyes on the road. "I won't hurt you."

She arched a brow. She hadn't wanted to mention the possibility of *hurt*, but now he'd brought it up. So…should she jump out? The rickshaw was moving at a quick clip, but nothing held her in the vehicle. If she jumped, though, she'd bruise something, maybe even break a bone on the pavement. And how could she compete in a national beauty pageant with skinned knees and elbows?

"I'm not afraid." She lifted her chin. "I just want to know where we're going."

Without another word Victor turned down a narrow residential street. A shiver climbed the ladder of her spine as he slowed his pace. Would he try to kidnap her now? Would he knock her over the head, tie her up, and hide her in one of these houses? She closed her eyes, imagining her frantic family on the evening news, tearfully telling a reporter that the unthinkable had happened—

Her eyes snapped open when the rickshaw stopped at a white house with green shutters. A seahorse adorned the wall by the door, and someone had painted a matching design on the mailbox.

"Here." Victor pulled the buggy onto a threadbare lawn. "My grandmother lives here."

"You want to visit your grandmother? Okay, I'll wait outside. Or maybe I'll walk out to the highway and try to hail a taxi—"

"Please." When Victor turned she looked into the depths of his dark eyes…and saw what she had not seen before.

Victor was no college student. He was a young man trying to make his way with limited intelligence and an oversized heart.

He glanced at the ground, then lifted one hand and tugged at the spikes of his hair. "My grandmother doesn't know us any more. Mom says Grandma thinks she's a young woman, so she cries for her sister. She's so lonely."

"But I don't see—"

"You look sorta like her picture—Ruby's, I mean. I saw you and knew you could make Grandma happy. For just a minute, will you say hello? Let her see you."

A thousand objections fluttered through Malena's mind. This was *crazy*; even simple-minded men could be dangerous. The national pageant would begin in less than six hours, and she needed that power nap. Besides, by this time Marcy Harcourt had probably broken out in hives.

The biggest problem, though, was rule number one, the decree that had been drummed into the contestants' heads ever since their arrival: any girl who slipped away from a pageant activity without permission would be immediately disqualified.

Being kidnapped wouldn't get Malena disqualified, but volunteering to visit this grandma would. The other girls would say she'd slipped out to whip up publicity; they'd think she'd arranged the entire abduction. After all, she was Miss Florida and this was her home turf. What better way to snag press attention than by staging a kidnapping just before the pageant? If she went into that house, they'd say she'd arranged to be caught playing angel of mercy just as the police pulled up.

Malena felt a wry smile twist her mouth. If she wanted to remain in the pageant, she had only one option: she needed to turn and run for the highway, leaving Victor to face the consequences of his actions. Already she could hear the distant wail of a siren. The police would be combing these streets soon, searching for a rickshaw, and they'd find it in a flash. This childlike, sweet young man would be arrested, tossed into jail, and his picture plastered on the cover of *People* and *Pageant Life*.

What sort of beauty queen would let that happen?

She shaded her eyes from the sun. "Pull the rickshaw into the garage, Victor. And have your mama call a taxi so I'll have a ride back to the hotel."

Relief shone in his smile. "You're not mad at me?"

"I'm not, but Ritchie will probably fire you."

"I can work another job. I am slow—" he tapped the side of his head—"but I am strong."

Malena gestured to the door. "Is your grandmother here?"

He nodded. "My mom sits with her."

Malena wiped her damp hands on her skirt, then went to the door and knocked. A moment later a middle-aged woman peered out from behind a security chain.

"Mom," Victor stepped onto the concrete porch, "I brought this lady to see Grandma. And you need to call a taxi."

"Son, what have you done now?" Victor's mother shook her head, then extended her hand. "I'm Irene."

"Malena. And it's nice to meet you."

When Irene opened the door, Malena stepped into a room that smelled of disinfectant and age, then spied the small woman propped up on the sofa. A black and white television droned in the corner, but the elderly woman's eyes were focused on some interior field of vision Malena couldn't even imagine.

"Victor," she eased into the room, "what is your Grandma's name?"

"Edna."

Malena walked forward and placed her hand on the old woman's arm. "Edna?" Slowly the wide eyes swiveled, then the woman's lips parted as joy lit her face.

Malena sank to the sofa as Edna reached up to touch her arms and shoulders. Soon age-spotted hands were feathering across her cheeks, her nose.

"Ruby," the woman whispered, her trembling fingers stroking Malena's hair. "Where have you been? I've been waiting a long time."

Malena couldn't speak. Tears rained from her eyes, melting her mascara and smearing the foundation and blush she had so carefully applied. What did it matter? Suddenly it seemed more important to spend an hour looking like Ruby than a year being Miss American Pride.

"I'm Malena," she finally managed to whisper.

"She won't understand, hon," Irene said, sinking into an easy chair. "The doctor told us we need to let her mind go where it will—we'll upset her if we try to correct her."

As Edna crooned a song, Malena pulled a card from her pocket and handed it to Irene. "Would you mind phoning that number for me? Tell the woman who answers that Malena Osborne will meet the group at the hotel. Oh—and tell her I'll be withdrawing."

Irene's brow quirked.

"It's okay," Malena assured her. "She'll know what you mean."

A drawerful of tiaras was more than enough; she could keep slinging hash to pay her tuition.

"Beautiful," Edna whispered. She held quivering fingers to her lips, then pressed them to Malena's cheek. "Ruby, you are so beautiful."

Malena felt her chin quiver as precious words rose on a wave of memory: *You should be known for the beauty that comes from within, the unfading beauty of a gentle and quiet spirit, which is so precious to God.*

Later this afternoon she would write a letter of resignation, pack her things, and return to school. But first she'd offer a prayer of repentance for allowing herself to forget that beauty had more to do with her heart than her appearance.

So that's exactly what she did.

*   *   *

ANGELA HUNT is the best-selling author of *The Tale of Three Trees*, *The Debt*, *The Note*, and many other titles for children and adults.

Eight of her novels have won Angel Awards from Excellence in Media. Hunt has also won two silver medals from ForeWord Magazine's book of the year award (for *The Justice* and *The Canopy*), and a Christy Award for *By Dawn's*

Early Light. She and her youth pastor-husband make their home in Florida with two mastiffs. In 2001, one of her pets was featured on *Live with Regis and Kelly* as the second-largest dog in America.

Visit her web page at www.angelahuntbooks.com.

Thanksgiving Break

Clay Jacobsen

The wind was picking up, sending sheets of rain across the darkened road and blanketing the car's windshield. Still several hours from home, Tracy Williams decided she'd better pull off the road.

She was exhausted, having already driven halfway across Tennessee from the state university in Knoxville. It was Thanksgiving break and the rigorous nursing program had taken its toll—Tracy was in great need of a few days off.

Through the slapping windshield wipers she spotted a blurred neon sign that read "Waffle House."

Perfect.

"What can I get for ya, miss?"

Tracy smiled at the waitress and turned the mug in front of her right-side-up. "Just some coffee, please."

"You got it. I'll be right back."

Tracy stretched, then leaned against the back of the booth. She rubbed her eyes. Making it home was going to be tough. She caught her reflection in the mirror on the other side of the booth—it wasn't a pretty sight. Her eyes were puffy and beet red, hiding their normally vibrant blue. Her blonde hair was flat and greasy, her make-up definitely in need of a touch-up.

"Here you go," the waitress offered, pouring the steaming black liquid into Tracy's cup.

"Thanks." Tracy grabbed a packet of sugar, pouring it into the cup and stirring it slowly with her spoon. She picked up the mug and brought it to her lips, blowing gently over the top.

The door to the café opened, sending a rush of cold air into the restaurant. Tracy looked up, catching a glimpse of a man as she took a small sip. He had to fight the wind to close the door behind him.

He was tall; Tracy guessed about six foot two, with short dark hair—about her age. She rated him a seven, not bad-looking, but nothing to write home about. His nose seemed a bit large for his face.

The stranger looked intently across the near-empty restaurant. Tracy looked down before his eyes landed on her.

She took a sip of coffee and what began as a warm sensation gliding down her throat turned into a chill when the stranger stepped toward her. Tracy kept her eyes on the table and began praying under her breath.

"I'm glad you came."

He had stopped right beside her. Tracy looked up. "Excuse me?"

Without invitation, he sat down across from her and smiled. "You know, with the storm and all, I'm glad you're here."

Tracy tilted her head, "I think you have me confused with somebody else."

"No, don't say that." He blinked rapidly. "We've planned this meeting for weeks."

Tracy didn't move.

He smiled. "I'm Thornberry Seven."

She shook her head. "I don't know what that means."

His face darkened for an instant, then his smile returned. "Oh, I get it. You're playing with me."

Her pulse quickened. She looked around the empty restaurant to see who might be able to help her if this guy went nuts.

"So what'll it be, Ladybug?" the stranger continued. "You want me to introduce myself properly?"

"Like I said," Tracy said, "I'm not who you think I am. I'm just driving through town trying to make my way home for Thanksgiving."

"No!"

His hand came down swiftly, landing open-palmed on the table. The silverware rattled and Tracy jumped.

She gulped in a breath of air and looked right at him. His eyes bore into her, the friendly glint replaced by an anger that was palpable. He blinked slowly and tilted his head. When he looked at her again, his expression had softened.

"I'm sorry," he said. "I didn't mean to frighten you."

"Look, I think—"

"Please," he interrupted. "Let me start over. My name's Rich, Rich Graham."

Tracy hesitated, looking toward the kitchen. Where was the waitress?

"Rich," Tracy turned back, "it's nice to meet you. But I really am a college student. I've got several hours still to drive. I just want to drink my coffee and get back on the road as soon as this storm settles."

Rich sat like a statue for several seconds, then leaned back into the booth and cleared his throat. His brow creased and his eyes turned black as he spread out his hands. "So what is it?"

Tracy didn't answer.

"Expecting Brad Pitt and now you don't like what you see, is that it?"

"No," Tracy responded firmly. "I'm not expecting anyone."

Rich leaned in close to Tracy, speaking in a harsh yet softened voice. "Liar."

Her heart skipped. She looked around for anyone that could help. No one appeared. "I'd like to be left alone, please."

"Alone!" Rich blurted out, anger returning like flames in his eyes. "You're Ladybug. We met in a chat room several months ago."

Tracy shook her head, sinking into the booth as he rambled on.

"You're a waitress at Applebees. Your name is Sally and you're twenty-five years old. You love movies—your favorite is *Steel Magnolias*—"

"Rich," Tracy interrupted. "I'm not Sally. I've never—"

"Yes, you are. You emailed me your picture!"

"No, I didn't," Tracy stated flatly. She thought for a second. "Do you have it with you?"

"No—yes!" He brightened. "It's in my truck. You'll see."

Rich bolted from the booth and headed for the door. Tracy scanned the diner. The only other occupants were an elderly couple sharing a piece of pie at a table in the corner.

She grabbed her purse and quickly placed a couple of dollars on the table-top before heading to the door. She looked out to the parking lot, spotting a white pick-up truck, but no sign of Rich. She pulled her keys out of her purse and held them in her hand—ready.

Through the downpour she saw the pick-up's interior lights illuminate. Tracy didn't hesitate. She quickly opened the café door and ran straight for her Honda Civic.

She stopped beside the driver's door and crouched low, keeping her eyes on the entrance to the restaurant.

The rain pelted her, soaking through her jeans and bouncing off her jacket. When she wiped the water away from her eyes, she spotted him.

He was heading back toward the café. Tracy hit the button on her key chain that unlocked her car then opened the door and climbed in. She closed the door beside her as quickly as she could—cursing Honda's feature that left the interior lights on for five seconds before fading slowly.

She kept her eyes trained on Rich's back, waiting for him to enter the restaurant before starting the car.

He stopped and turned around. Tracy ducked, but the dome light was still on—shining brightly over her blonde hair.

Rich spotted her as she turned the key. The Honda fired to life.

He began running straight at her. Tracy screamed, slammed the gearshift into reverse and pushed on the gas pedal. The tires spun on the wet pavement as Rich reached the front hood. Tracy couldn't help but look straight into his eyes—they were inflamed, the distortion of the wet windshield making him look like a wild wolf locked onto his prey.

Finally the tires took hold and the car lurched backward, throwing Rich facedown onto the pavement. Tracy reached over to hit the power door lock; her hand was shaking so badly it took two tries before she heard the comforting sound of the locks clamping into place.

Suddenly her body slammed into the back of the seat, her head snapping back. She watched as the rearview mirror filled with the image of Rich's white pick-up.

She'd smashed his truck!

Tracy found herself gulping breaths—too quickly. She was on the verge of hyperventilating.

No time to think—Rich was up again, heading toward her and screaming.

She forced the gearshift into drive and pounced on the gas again. She swerved to the right, just missing Rich as he leaped out of the way.

"Sally, wait!" Tracy heard, but she kept her focus on swinging the steering wheel to the left to keep the car under control. She kept accelerating, hitting the main road and speeding off into the night. The rain came down in such torrents it was impossible to keep track of the white line marking the middle of the road.

Tracy was shaking. She forced herself to take a deep breath, trying to fend off the effects of oxygen depravation.

"Lord, don't let him follow me. Please, God!" Her voice trembled. She didn't dare take her eyes off the road to look into the rearview mirror. She didn't need to. The reflection of a pair of headlights flashed across her eyes.

She turned right at the first road, passing a large sign: "Welcome to The Hermitage, home of Andrew Jackson."

Great, she thought. *There'll be nobody there at this hour. God, I could use a little help here!*

The road turned. She managed the first curve but halfway into the second the car skidded. She couldn't correct it on the wet surface and the car flew off the road.

The Honda landed sideways on two wheels in a drainage creek. Tracy sat wide-eyed, slipping into shock. Then water started rushing into the car around her feet—forcing Tracy into action.

Reaching for the latch on her seatbelt, she realized that half the front windshield was under a five-foot torrent of muddy water. Fighting the surge of panic rising from her gut, Tracy pushed herself out from under the steering wheel and reached toward the passenger door.

It was locked.

The water was at her waist—the engine had stalled. The lights of the car cast an eerie glow around her. She flipped up the power lock switch—nothing happened. She frantically pushed the window switch, trying to roll the window down and crawl out—still nothing. Fighting back the nightmare of drowning inside her own car, Tracy pushed against the window, praying for intervention. Then she noticed the lock on the right side of the door and almost laughed at her stupidity. Reaching out, she pulled up on the knob.

The door was unlocked, yet it wouldn't budge. She pushed straight up with all her might, groaning like a weightlifter until the door finally popped open. Fighting through the pouring rain she made her way out and sat on top of the right front panel. The dirty water rushed around her, any slip and she'd be swept downstream with little hope of survival. All she had to do was jump to the shore, just a few feet away.

"Sally," Tracy heard, "Hold on, I'm coming!"

Tracy looked up as a flash of lightning struck overhead. There stood Rich, arms outstretched as if he would be her savior.

Not today.

He started down the embankment. A second bolt of lightning slashed across the sky and Rich came to an abrupt halt.

Tracy didn't hesitate. She turned and jumped into the rushing water.

"Noooo!" she heard from behind her, but she didn't give it a second thought. The water was even more powerful than she'd expected and she found it impossible to keep her head above water.

She had to get to shore, and quickly. She pointed her body toward the side of the creek and stroked furiously. For every inch she gained sideways, she moved twenty yards downstream. At least she was that much farther away from Rich.

As she gulped for air, a flash of lightning lit the bank ahead where the stream took a turn. She reached hard with her right hand and pulled at the water, trying to break free when it turned. When she was a few feet from shore, her chest smashed into a large boulder.

Her breath left her and her head sunk under the water. Panic washed over her; she gasped for air that wasn't there. Her hand reached out one last time but found nothing.

Her vision began to collapse inward as the darkness overwhelmed her. She couldn't fight anymore. She just wanted to rest, to succumb to the inviting blackness. Tracy imagined a hand grasping onto hers and in the deep recesses of her mind, she envisioned holding on like a mad pit bull.

Rich stood entrenched on the side of the creek—staring ahead. He hadn't noticed the sheriff's car that pulled up behind him, lights flashing. His eyes stayed glued in front of him, reacting to what he'd seen when the second flash of lightning struck. Standing on either side of Tracy's car, half submerged in the water, were two huge men staring directly at Rich with their arms crossed. When the lightning faded, it seemed to Rich as if the men continued to glow. Their eyes were like fire, challenging him to continue his chase. He dared not move until their images faded…which happened in the same instant the sheriff deputy behind him yelled, "Don't move!"

Tracy heaved—coughing up what seemed like a gallon of muddy floodwater. She gasped, savoring the intake of air. Her lungs ached. Her chest felt like a sledgehammer had slammed into it.

She rolled over on her back and moaned, letting the rain wash over her. She was alive—barely. A strong hand reached out and pushed her hair away from her face.

She opened her eyes.

"Are you feeling better, miss?"

Kneeling above her was the smiling face of the sheriff's deputy who had pulled her from the raging creek. Behind him was the café where it had all started.

"How—" Tracy sputtered.

"Cindy, your waitress, called us as soon as you left the Waffle House," the officer explained. "Another deputy is up the road where your car went into the wash. He radioed that you jumped in the creek—I got here just as you floated by."

"What about—"

"The man that chased you? We ran a check on him—turns out he's wanted for questioning in connection with a string of date rapes of young women he's met online and lured into meeting him."

Tracy sighed and looked back at the rushing water. "Thank you so much."

"You're welcome. I'm glad you're OK. But if you ask me," the deputy continued, "to come out of that creek alive, you should be thanking the good Lord above."

So that's exactly what she did.

*   *   *

Living and working in Southern California, CLAY JACOBSEN has been directing television programs for over twenty years. His credits include shows such as *The Jerry Lewis Telethon, Entertainment Tonight, The Other Half, Dr. Laura, Prime Time Country* and *Dennis Miller*. Clay's theme in writing is: Novels that challenge the spirit. *The Lasko Interview, Circle of Seven,* and *Interview with the Devil* are thrillers that delve behind the scenes of the entertainment industry.

With his brother, Wayne, Clay also co-wrote a non-fiction book entitled *Authentic Relationships: Discover the Lost Art of One Anothering*. To find out more about these books visit: www.clayjacobsen.com.

Priorities

Yvonne Lehman

The wind was picking up. I heard it laughing in the trees just before the phone rang. Jake's gaze met mine in the mirror and my hand didn't complete the task of putting on my diamond earring. *Please don't answer.*

Jake glanced at the caller ID. "I have to get it, RosaLee." He hurried toward his study.

Don't let this night be spoiled. I walked into the hallway. Looking up, I saw Len coming down the stairs with his eyes full of apprehension.

I tried to smile. Len would change into his Hamlet costume at school. He looked so grown up, with his suit coat tossed over one shoulder, his dark hair combed to perfection. "I'm so proud of you, Honey." I tried to cover the sound of Jake's voice in the study.

Len nodded. "Thanks." He attempted a smile. "You look great, Mom."

"Thank you," I replied. But we both knew looks was not what concerned us. We were pretending everything would work out.

We knew it wouldn't when Jake came out with regret in his eyes. "The only time Heneson can meet with me is tonight. Like I've told you, if I don't make this sale I could go bankrupt."

Financially is not the only way one can be bankrupt, I could have said.

Jake looked truly sorry. But then, he'd had years of practice.

Len had years of practice, too—saying, "I understand." However, after his freshman year, "I understand" sounded like an accusation. Jake had explained, over and over, that he had to make a living for the family. He couldn't take off every time Len was in a school play.

I braced myself for Len's disappointment. But it wasn't disappointment that came from my son's mouth.

"I don't want you there," Len blurted. "I knew you'd get out of it. Why don't you tell the truth instead of pretending you have an important meeting. You just don't want to go."

I touched Len's arm. He shouldn't talk to his father like that. He shouldn't get upset before a performance. But he shrugged away. His words were full of hurt. "I'm not the son you want. You never wanted me in the first place."

Jake reached for the door casing, reeling from the onslaught. "How can you say such a thing?"

"How?" Len blared. "You said it. In plain English, in black and white."

"Never," Jake said. "I don't know what you're talking about."

"No?" Len brushed past his dad, strode to a file drawer and pulled out a sheet of paper. Approaching his dad, he tossed the paper at him. Jake tried to grab it, but it fell to the floor.

"See," Len blurted. "I can't even throw a piece of paper hard enough to reach you." He rushed out the front door.

Jake picked up the paper. His red face paled.

"What is it?"

Jake read aloud.

Dear Jimmy,

I'm not a man of many words and I didn't tell you enough what was in my heart. I had so many plans for us. I was going to teach you to play ball. We would go to games and cheer for the team. We'd take long hikes. Fix a bicycle. Build things. You would play in Little League and I'd be the coach. I'd teach you how to dunk a basketball, hit a soccer ball with your head and knees, kick a football, catch a baseball. You would make me proud.

Son, I don't know how I'll make it without you. I'm trying real hard, but I cry every night because I miss you so. I don't know why God let that disease take over your body. I'll just have to ask him when I get to heaven. In the meantime, be a good boy. Play ball with the angels. Knock a home run for me.

I'll be seeing you. And remember I love you.

Dad

Jake looked at me with tears streaking his face. "I wrote this the night of Jimmy's funeral. I haven't thought about it in years. Didn't even know where it was."

Like a light going on, I realized when Len had found the letter. The summer he was fourteen, he'd decided he would learn how to work in the machine shop like his dad. Doing something to please his dad had meant everything. Len had started helping his dad clean out the files. Jake told him what to discard and what to keep. Len had worked with his dad for half a day. During lunch, he'd been sullen and quiet. Later, he told me he had decided not to be a machinist.

I knew Len's interests weren't sports or machines. Through the years, Jake had tried to play ball with Len, but our boy grew frustrated because he couldn't catch and didn't want to tackle. He'd dodge a soccer ball instead of hit it with his head or body. He was interested in the piano, so I taught him to play. He could sing, draw, and had started drama with Primary Players in third grade.

Jake and Len were so different. They had tried. Len had tried that summer he was fourteen. He must have found the letter then, because after that he no longer tried to gain his dad's favor. We labeled it "teenage rebellion." Len didn't turn to drugs or alcohol, but got closer to God. Jake and I were pleased, but the relationship between father and son worsened. Jake worked harder. Len became more active in school and church activities.

Now Jake fell on his knees, crying out, "Oh God, how do I let my son know how much I love him?"

"Tell him. Show him by going to his play. That's all Len and I ever wanted from you. Not—" I gestured with my hands—"not this house, or the cars, or the maid, or the beautiful clothes."

Seeing the crushed look on his face, I almost relented and told him I didn't mean it. I was rejecting him, like my mother rejected me when she placed me in the orphanage where Jake and I both grew up.

He rose from his knees. "Why do you think I worked hard to give you—" he spread his hands like I had—"all this?"

"I know why, Jake. Because you love me. But I would love you if we lived in a tent. Remember when we camped out on our honeymoon?"

"That's easy to say when you're on the receiving end," he said. "I'm the breadwinner. You have my love. All this shows it. Now, you're asking that we live in a tent?"

At age twenty-one I could live in a tent. At age forty-two, I could not. But I could get a job. Realizing I wasn't as eager for poverty as I pretended, I shifted blame to Jake. "This is the biggest night of our son's school life. This is the senior play and he has the lead role. He needs his dad to acknowledge that."

Leaving Jake slumped on the couch, I grabbed the car keys and walked out into the wind that cooled my burning cheeks. Guilt plagued me. I knew no man had ever worked harder than Jake. But in the past few years he had over-extended. He needed to sell one of the shops in order to maintain our lifestyle.

I would behave as usual and sit in that reserved seat beside the empty one my husband should occupy. As I drove, I told myself not to cry, but my vision became blurred.

It cleared as I rounded the curve of the Richard Petty Bridge on I-40 when I glanced in the rear-view mirror and saw blue lights flashing. I speeded up to pass the cars on my right, then pulled over so the police could get by. I got over, and he got over, in fast pursuit. That's when his siren began to echo across the mountains.

After I pulled off the road, the policeman came to my window. "Evening, RosaLee." He was a neighbor who lived a block away. He grinned. "We have one bridge named after a famous racecar driver. You really think we need another?"

When I told him my story of Len being in the school play I burst into tears. He softened and only gave me a warning ticket.

When the play was half over, Jake slipped in and sat beside me. I should have been glad but I could only think, *Business first, family last.*

At intermission I remained seated. "Short meeting?"

"I didn't go, RosaLee."

"Then what took you so long to get here?"

He sighed. "Somebody took my car keys so I had to borrow the moped from the boy next door."

"You...rode here on a moped?"

"Had no choice." He took a piece of paper from his suit coat pocket and thrust it into my hand.

I read.

❧

Len,

Forgive me for being such an idiot. I never compared you with Jimmy. I thought I was supposed to teach you to play ball and go fishing. I thought those were manly things. But you were afraid of the ball. You didn't like killing worms or cutting open a dead fish.

But you had talents I couldn't begin to have. You took to the piano like a fish takes to water. You're so smart and try to talk to me about history and science and the Count of Monte Crisco and I know nothing about those things. I was not in those advanced classes. I barely scraped by. I was good with my hands. It's all I knew. I wanted to give you a home and all the things I never had.

I guess I took for granted you knew how much I loved you. I admire your creativity and respect your dedication to the Lord. I've always thought you were special.

I wanted to be a success so you would admire me. I look back now and think about what I'd want in a dad. I would just want him near me, to talk to me, to love me. I can't talk about some of the things you talk about, but I will take time from now on to listen.

I love you, son. I never wanted you to replace Jimmy. He will always have a place in my heart. But I wrote that letter as a final goodbye. Oh, I think of him, but I've never compared him with you. I even forgot about that letter. I thought it was lost years ago.

But this is about you and me, Son. I'm not good with words. But as God is my witness, I love you. You're my life. You're my boy.

Will you give me another chance?

Dad

I looked at Jake and saw the pain and uncertainty in his eyes. "It's perfect," I said. "I'll take it backstage."

When the lights went down and I returned to my seat, I noticed Jake holding a cellophane-wrapped package. My husband, whose hands were often grease-stained, held roses until the end of the play. As the curtain fell and lifted again, Jake approached the stage with the armload of roses. He held them out to Len.

Len stepped forward and took the flowers. I saw his lips say *I love you too* before he stepped back to the row of actors.

The audience gave the actors a standing ovation. My heart did the same for my husband and my son.

We attended the party for the actors and their families. I reveled in the glances my husband and son flashed at each other. Jake proudly accepted compliments about his son. Len kept smiling.

When we got home, Len took the letter from his pocket. "Dad," he said, "this is the most beautiful piece of writing I've ever read." He took a deep breath. "That's all I ever wanted. Just to have you care what I'm doing. I felt like I couldn't live up to your standards."

"Oh, Son," Jake said. "You've exceeded my standards. But it would be okay if you didn't." He put his arm around Len's shoulders. "You're my boy, my life. I'm proud of you. And I love you more than I can say."

"You have said it, Dad." They fell into a tight embrace.

Finally they stepped away. "Keep that letter to remind you," Jake said.

"I'll never lose this letter, Dad. Or my respect and love for you. I know how hard you've worked for us. And I know what tonight may have cost you."

Jake teared. "I've regained my son. That means more than anything."

Later, Jake and I were in our bedroom. The phone rang. I glanced at the Caller ID. "It's Mr. Heneson."

Jake shook his head. "Doesn't matter. I called and cancelled the meeting. If he buys, let's make our lives more worthwhile—maybe go into needy areas and help other people. You know, we talked about that when we were young. I don't ever want money to replace love again. I feel your respect and love, Rosa-Lee. I felt Len's love tonight."

Jake smiled. "You know, this is all a case of mistaken identity. I'm not a lover of money. I'm just a simple man who loves his wife and son."

We kept talking, paying no attention to the answering machine taking Mr. Heneson's message.

"It hasn't been bad, Jake. We just haven't communicated well."

Jake nodded and grinned. "If he doesn't buy, I could still manage to get you the prettiest tent around."

I lay awake for a long time, thanking God for what we had learned. After Jake's light breathing started, I went into the study, closed the door, and listened to Mr. Heneson's message.

"Jake," he said. "For several weeks, I couldn't figure out why you would sell your business. Oh, I understand a dropping economy, but wondered if you were telling me everything. You said you'd overextended with building a bigger shop, a bigger warehouse, and hiring more employees. But when you said, 'Take it or leave it. I'm going to my son's school play,' you put me to shame. You see, I was supposed to attend a dinner party with my wife tonight. Thanks for canceling and reminding me of what my priorities should be. Could you call me tomorrow?"

I returned to the bedroom. Jake stirred. "You want to know what Mr. Heneson said?"

Jake shrugged. "I gave it to the Lord. You just decide what color tent you want. I love you."

I had never felt it so much, nor had truer words ever been spoken when I replied, "You're my hero, Jake. I love you so much."

He turned toward me. "Then shut up and kiss me, the hero said to his wife."

His lips touched mine as I was thinking, *So that's exactly what she did.*

✳   ✳   ✳

YVONNE LEHMAN, a best-selling author of forty novels, resides in the panoramic mountains of western North Carolina. She founded and directed the Blue Ridge Christian Writers Conference for seventeen years. She now directs the Blue Ridge Mountains Christian Writers Conference, sponsored by LifeWay/Ridgecrest Conference Center in Ridgecrest, NC (25 miles east of Asheville).

She has won numerous awards including The Dwight L. Moody Award for Excellence in Christian Writing, the Inspirational Romance Award from *Romantic Times*, several awards from The National League of American Pen Women, the Booksellers' Best Award, Inspirational Romance Reader's Award, and National Readers Choice Award. Her latest book is a women's fiction title, *Coffee Rings* (Barbour). Her website is www.yvonnelehman.com.

Salzburg Sunrise

Gail Gaymer Martin

The wind was picking up as the summer shower splatted from the gray morning sky to the cobblestones of the Dom Platz. Sophie Blair pulled the umbrella closer, then stepped into the Salzburg cathedral doorway for cover.

She'd looked forward to this day but disappointment settled over her—eight-thirty and Jon still hadn't arrived. She'd sensed God's blessing on her amazing trip to Austria, but at this moment, her spirit had dampened like the weather.

As if God responded, Sophie's hopes lifted when she saw a young man striding across the platz toward her. His umbrella hovered above his head, but when she caught a glimpse of him, she noted his photographs didn't do him justice.

"Jon?" She stepped from the Dom's entrance and waved.

"Yes," he said, a quizzical look sliding across his face.

"It's me. Sophie." She rushed forward, wrapping one arm around his neck as their umbrellas dueled overhead. "I'm thrilled to meet you finally."

He studied her face. "So am I."

Her chest tightened until she realized his confusion. "You look different than your photos, too," she said. "Snapshots rarely do justice."

He laughed. "True," he said, his German accent adding a depth to his voice. He stepped back. "So?"

His question puzzled her. "You promised to show me the city. Last evening when I arrived, I was too tired to venture out."

"A tour of Salzburg. Certainly." He gazed across the square. "We will head over the bridge and begin there."

Despite his smile, Sophie sensed an aloofness she'd never expected from Jon. He'd always been friendly and spirited. "Am I keeping you from something?"

He gave her a surprised look. "No. Later I have a responsibility, but not now."

His comment made her curious, but he didn't expound and she didn't ask.

While they walked, the sun peeked from behind the clouds as the rain slowed, then stopped, offering Sophie the promise of a brighter day. "Do you realize I might never have met you if the Glory Ringers hadn't arranged this trip?"

"That would have been too bad." His warm smile faded. "But who are the Glory Ringers?"

"The handbell group. I've told you about them. It's our European tour, and we're here for the Salzburg Music Festival. I gave you all the details in my email."

His eyes glinted. "You will perform when?"

"Tomorrow. Four o'clock at St. Peter's Church."

"I will be there," he said, glinting a grin.

"Wonderful," she said.

While they followed the river, they talked as Sophie studied his handsome features, amazed at the feelings that charged through her despite her attempt to quell them. Since high school, she and Jon had written pen pal letters until computers replaced the need for stamps—friends and nothing more—but seeing him in person created a spark Sophie hadn't expected.

Jon seemed quiet as they crossed the bridge, but on the other side he brightened, sharing the history of the Mirabellgarten and palace. He bought them drinks at the snack bar nearby, and they sat on a wooden bench, watching the fountain splay into the oval pond.

"Now, tell me about yourself," Jon said, his handsome face brightened by the now unsullied sunshine.

"Why? You've heard it all."

"But not face to face." He slipped his arm behind her and rested it on the bench back.

The closeness did something to her senses, and she longed to tell him what strange feelings she'd felt since they met. "I'll tell you, if you do the same. You seem different than I expected."

Jon's finger brushed against her shoulder. "Is that bad?"

"Not at all. It's—" The words were lost in the sparkle of his deep blue eyes.

"Later, *Liebchen*, I'll tell you all about me."

His words scuttled through her, and Sophie repeated stories he'd already heard about her life growing up in a Chicago suburb, her love of music, her faith, and her job as a secretary. Nothing glamorous, but it was her life, and he'd always been a bright spot when she heard the words, "You've got mail."

As she spoke, they wandered back to the Salzach River where they ate lunch at a busy café with wood-plank floors and long pine tables. Finished, Jon rose. "Are you ready for the many stairs to the Nonneburg Abbey?"

With Jon, she felt ready for anything.

He slipped his arm around her waist and used his umbrella as a walking stick. As they climbed the broad stone steps, Sophie looked out over the lovely city of Salzburg with its domes and gray slate rooftops.

A breeze ruffled the foliage, making patterns on the stone stairs, and Sophie's heart fluttered with joy. Jon smiled and drew her closer, their footsteps matching as they climbed. At the abbey door, they left the bright sunlight for the gloomy interior, but soon Sophie's eyes adjusted and she viewed the peaceful chapel. A postulate entered to sweep the floor, and Sophie followed Jon back into the summer air where he paused. "The sunset is beautiful from here. I hope you see it before you leave."

"I would love to see it," she said, hoping he was about to extend an invitation.

"Unfortunately, tonight I have other plans." He dug into his pocket and drew out a card, then held it in his long, slender fingers.

"Perhaps another time," she said, weighted by disappointment.

As Sophie waited, she realized he had something to say that wasn't coming easily. For a moment, she froze with expectation. Did he want to end their friendship? Perhaps a lady friend was jealous of his pen pal. "What is it, Jon?"

"I have to leave you now. I'm sorry, but here's a ticket for tonight's concert in the Prince's Chambers at the top of Hohensalzburg." He motioned toward the fortress.

Sophie examined the ticket. Mozart Concert at 7:30. She loved chamber music, but—"You want me to meet you there?"

"Please. I'll explain all—"

Her cell phone cut him off with its familiar melody. Sophie dug through her handbag to locate it, then said hello.

"Sophie, I'm so sorry about this confusion, but I'm off earlier than I expected. Could we meet for dinner?"

She gaped at the phone. "Jon?" As she said the name, she peered at the man standing beside her.

"Who else?" His chuckle echoed through the earpiece. "I do not enjoy working on Saturday, but that is how it is. Is dinner acceptable?"

Their conversation blurred, but she agreed, then turned off the cell phone, her mind boiling with questions, her emotions bubbling with confusion. "Who are you?" she asked, her cheek ticking with anger.

"I'm Johann, but not the one you expected."

"Then why did you do this?"

He eyed his watch again. "I must go now, Sophie. Meet me tonight at the concert, I'll explain everything then. Forgive me for not waiting, but I have responsibilities." He scooted past her and bounded down the stone steps.

Mortified, Sophie's eyes blurred with tears. She'd spent the day with a stranger, sharing her life story, allowing him to hold her hand, and feeling...The sensations rolled over her. He'd acted thoughtful and generous, making her laugh and feel special. He'd been wonderful. Yet how had she been so dense?

When Sophie reached the bottom of the steps, she paused to get her bearings. She spotted the roof of St. Peter's Church. She ambled through the narrow streets and when she entered the dimly lit church, she stood a moment before sliding into a pew.

As she struggled with her thoughts, Sophie relived the day, angry at the stranger. Yet she'd been the one to jump into his arms with her greeting. Her gaze lifted to the amazing stained glass windows and God's Word filled her mind. *Do not judge and you will not be judged. Forgive, and you will be forgiven.*

Jon—Johann—said he'd explain later, but there would be no later. How could she trust a man who hadn't admitted her mistake from the beginning? Still, the Lord's message filled her mind. *Do not judge. Forgive.*

Sophie rose and hurried back to her hotel. She changed her clothes and freshened her makeup, then headed for the hotel lobby. As she descended the last set of stairs, she saw her pen pal. He looked exactly as she'd seen him in photographs. How could she have allowed herself to be duped?

"Jon," she said, running to greet him.

His face brightened and recognition settled in his eyes. "Sophie. At long last."

He wrapped his arms around her; his rosy cheek pressed against hers. Jabbering like old friends, they ambled to the restaurant. The time flew as they relived the years of emails, but foremost in Sophie's mind was the stranger, the other Jon who'd stepped into her life.

"I need to make a confession," Sophie said, unable to keep her mistake a secret.

"Confession?"

"I thought you'd stood me up today."

"Why?"

"I thought you meant eight this morning."

"Oh, Sophie, I'm so sorry."

"And that's not all." She told him about meeting Johann, her emotions, and what had transpired. Finally she pulled out the ticket. "He gave me this and asked me to meet him tonight."

Jon checked the ticket, then eyed the time. "You will have to hurry."

"But what do you think? He's a stranger. He let me think he was you."

"Not really. Jon is his name."

"His name is Johann."

"Yes, that's Jon in English," he said, then paused. "Sophie, let me see the ticket again."

He studied the smaller print, then beckoned her to read it. "Johann Braun," he said. "He's a fine concert pianist."

"Johann Braun?" Her thoughts rattled. She'd told him about the Glory Ringers and her trip to Austria as if she had accomplished a real musical feat. He was renowned. "No. It couldn't be."

"I'm certain it could. I hear he is a fine man and I know he's an amazing musician."

Do not judge. "You think I should go?"

"Definitely, my friend. I'll see you tomorrow at your concert."

Her concert...and Johann Braun said he'd attend. Her pulse skipped.

"You'd better run, Sophie, or you'll be late." He rose and tossed his Euros on the table beside the bill. "Let me take you the shortest route. You will ride the funicular to the top and then walk many flights of stairs."

He steered her outside and clasped her arm, nearly dragging her along the busy street. The fortress grew nearer and she could see spotlights on the towering walls and the lighted windows at the top. "I go up there?"

"Yes. To the top."

At the funicular, she waved goodbye and found a seat on the mountainside tram that would take her to the fortress grounds. The car jarred, then moved up the hill. At the top, she hurried to the fortress entrance and bounded up the many stairs.

Five flights up, she paused, panting. Why was she running? She was a foolish woman pursuing a man who gave her a concert ticket. Yet she sensed God's words in her ear. *There is a time for every purpose under heaven.* Was this her time? Her purpose?

Music echoed along the corridor. Sophie slipped inside and found her seat near the front. The string quartet finished and Sophie's heart stopped as Johann stepped into the light. He spotted her and his face glowed like the thousands of gilded bosses that studded the ceiling.

The room hushed as Johann's fingers rested on the keys. The music began, subtle and soft, building, moving in arpeggios and chords—dolorous to dolce, staccato to legato, powerful, sweet. When the last chord faded, the audience rose as bravos filled the air. Johann bowed and left the stage as Sophie burst upward, applauding wildly, her heart thundering.

At the intermission, Johann found her. "Shall we go? We have much to talk about."

"We do." His inquiring eyes tugged at her heart strings. "It's wonderful, but I'd rather talk."

His gentle look eased her frustration as they made their way down the stairs. Then nearing the funicular, Johann hesitated. "I must apologize for my masquerade today. At first, I thought I should know you."

Sophie's spirit lifted.

"But as we talked and I knew you had mistaken me for someone else, I could not say goodbye. You captured my interest. You are a beautiful woman, Sophie, but even more, you have a warm and spirited heart."

"Thank you," she said, uncomfortable with his compliments.

"You must understand I rarely meet people like others do. I never know if someone is seeking my company because of who I am...or who they want me to be. With you, I had no doubt. You cannot hide your feelings. I could see you enjoyed my company for me. I wasn't the Jon you sought, but I was the Jon with whom you laughed and shared your stories. You moved my heart."

His words were a balm. "I was embarrassed and angry, but I felt as if we were old friends even though we had just met."

"*Ja*, and now I will talk about my dreams and my travels. You're from Chicago, and I will be in Chicago in September. I will see you then, I hope."

"I hope," she said as her heart thrummed.

He took her hand, and they wandered the streets sharing their joys and sorrows. Very late they stopped for coffee. When the streets had quieted and only the stars lit the way, Johann drew her closer.

"We missed the sunset from the abbey, but we could watch the sunrise."

Wisdom cautioned Sophie, but her heart said yes. When they reached the top, a faint coral hue peaked from the horizon, then heightened to shades of fiery orange and burnished gold. They stood in silence as Sophie sorted through all that had happened that day.

"God is good," Johann said. "His creation is breathtaking." He turned to face her. "And so are you, Liebchen. I am honored to know you."

"I'm honored, too, Johann. I'm breathless—the sunrise, the city below, and you beside me."

"We have many days, Sophie. Hopefully years, if God wills." He drew her toward him.

Her heart swelled with the look in his eyes and she tilted her chin upward, waiting and hoping.

Then he caressed her cheek. "I would be honored if you would let me kiss you good morning."

Sophie wanted that, too. So that's exactly what she did.

*   *   *

Award-winning author GAIL GAYMER MARTIN writes romance, romantic suspense, and women's fiction for Steeple Hill and Barbour Publishing. She's the author of *The Christmas Kite* and *Michigan: A Novel*. She has twenty-nine books in print with over a million copies sold. Visit her web site at www.gailmartin.com.

One Lost Day

Cindy Martinusen

The wind was picking up.

He paced by covered windows, hearing the sound of palm trees clapping thick hands together. The blankets over the windows puffed as if a great monster breathed in and out. Blankets over windows were futile attempts to bring safety to this room.

The knock sounded again.

He stopped at the door.

"I have towels, sir." The hotel maid wasn't driven away as easily this time. "I need to check mini bar."

"Do not disturb me."

Wearily he leaned his forehead against the door. He nearly covered his face, then pulled his hands away as if his own skin would burn.

Finally, he heard the maid's footsteps and the sound of a cart wheeling away. He turned, sliding to the worn carpet where he pulled his legs close against himself. His no-wrinkle pants were wrinkled, and his tie dangled loose around his neck. His dress shirt had dark stains in the armpits—evidence of the humidity that finally passed with the afternoon. He guessed it was afternoon by the softened light edging around his black-out attempts. On other trips, he'd be sitting in meetings, or doing business that had seemed important at the time.

But this wasn't just another trip.

More time passed and another knock, only feet above where his head rested against the door.

"I wish to be alone," he called out.

"Sir, this is hotel manager. You have been in room for three days."

So three days, then. Part of him believed it had been longer. But what were days to him? Even hearing the word *days* brought a stab of panic.

"May we bring you meal, fresh towels and bedding? We require check of the mini bar, sir."

"Why not tomorrow?"

"Sir, you have phone messages."

What does it matter now?

"Excuse me, sir? Did you hear?"

"Please, I have work. Tomorrow—come back tomorrow."

Glancing up, he noticed the light had grown subtly darker. More passages of time. Around the room, he took inventory. His suitcase still zipped closed on the bed, one water bottle open, some food pulled from the mini bar but nothing touched.

So I haven't eaten in three days. Imagine that.

His body had that generic middle-aged businessman look—a little thick in the middle, even lacking three days nourishment. He considered touching his face, feeling for the changes, but his hand shook at every approach.

"Come quickly, darkness," he whispered. Except now that he'd given the hotel manager a time, he'd have to let them in tomorrow. Vaguely he remembered checking into this hotel in Manila. The Philippines, that's where he was. How strange that he could be anywhere right now. He'd come by taxi from the airport, rushed to the front desk. Then he felt the frantic panic that built inside, saw the stares, oh, the many stares.

There came a sudden tap against the wall, not the door this time. He followed the next taps to above the headboard. He pressed his ear to the wall, then jumped back when a voice said, "Hello?"

He sat very still on the bed, but it creaked slightly.

"I know you're in there. These walls are thinner than anyone would hope in a hotel. This isn't the States, though of course you know that. How silly of me."

Suddenly he recalled a door opening and movement in another room. Was that yesterday or before? He'd paid little attention; he'd known very little at all.

"Sorry, but I overheard you talking earlier. So I know you're in there."

Finally, he tossed out, "Who are you? What do you want?"

"I'm from the States too. Name is Maggie."

"How do you know I'm from the States?"

"You speak American-sounding English—big clue, you know."

Suddenly a thought. "When did you arrive?"

"Same flight as you."

"What do you mean, same flight? How would you know?"

"There were few white guys on the plane, then I saw you in the hotel lobby when I arrived."

He felt ice through the veins. "You saw me?"

"Well, sort of. The baseball hat and your head bent like a criminal, it was hard to miss you, but hard to really see you, too."

His mind raced with details. Could there be more like him? Wandering around, hiding in dark rooms, terrified as to what came next. "But...are you okay? Since the flight. Why are you still in your room?" Then he added as if he'd known all along, "It's been three days, you know."

"I'm sick."

"Did you say you're sick?"

"I think food poisoning from the clam chowder in San Francisco. I've been in my room for days."

He whispered, "I don't think it was food poisoning."

"What? I couldn't understand that."

"Are you sure it's food poisoning? I think it's something else."

"I'm pretty sure—want the sordid details? Why?"

"Cause something happened to me. I lost a day."

"What? I'm having trouble hearing. You lost a day?"

Then it came rushing back and he was telling her the story. Why not? He hadn't spoken to a soul since it began. Who was this Maggie anyway, but a stranger with no connection to him.

"It started before the flight. Something after me, it chased my car over the Golden Gate Bridge right after I left home. I kept looking outside, thinking maybe it was some terrorist plane swooping toward the bridge. I'm not crazy; this was real, more real than anything."

He kept telling it. The flight schedule and feelings that something ominous was about to happen.

"So how did you lose a day?" Maggie asked.

"I've figured this out. We left San Francisco at night and refueled in Hawaii, but with the time change, we were still in November twenty-second. Then we came to the International Date Line, probably before it turned to November twenty-third in the South Pacific. So we jumped right over that day."

"You'll gain it on the flight back."

"No, not really. You see, I skipped November twenty-third completely. I never lived it. What if my birthday was November twenty-third? What if that was the date I was supposed to die? I'll never have lived that day. None of us on the flight did. And you're sick. Maybe all of us have this. Maybe the Death Angel came and we skipped the day. Maybe the plane was supposed to crash or—"

"I don't know if that's accurate. We might have lived part of November twenty-third."

"Maybe, but I don't think so and it doesn't matter. It changed me."

His voice went hoarse as his hands came inches from his face—to the physical horror of all that had happened in the last days. "I glanced at my reflection on the way off the plane. It looked strange, like someone else. People stared. Then at customs, the guy kept looking at my passport, then at me. Said it didn't look like me, that I looked like someone from the *Alien* movies. He nearly didn't let me in."

"What is your name?"

"Charlie," he said, then stopped. Why did she want to know? Suddenly he knew she believed none of this story.

The phone rang, making him jump. Charlie backed away, noticing the red message light was beeping too.

"Aren't you going to answer?" she called between rings.

Suddenly, he knew. This was part of it. "Maggie" on the other side of the wall, the phone call, the messages already there, the hotel maid and manager. He glanced around, expecting to view a camera from the ceiling. Then, springing for the door, he flung it open, anticipating people waiting for him, police perhaps, men in black coats.

Empty. This was his chance. His feet moved slower than he willed them to go. Behind him he heard a door open and the woman call, "Charlie, wait! Come back!"

The elevator didn't open, so he rushed for the stairs. Down steps and through the hallway, that oppressive cloud chased on his heels or something more, something worse. He hit the sidewalk, overwhelmed by the noise of Manila, cars packing the street. The night was coming and coming fast. Not knowing where to go, he just ran. *Maybe I was abducted by aliens. Maybe I got food poisoning and it affected my brain. Maybe I'm dead and this is hell.*

He searched for what pursued him even as he darted around people. Couples, families, teenagers—some had smiles that faded to questions. He kept running. Passing a building, he spotted a giant clock glaring down. The arms tapped out seconds that he didn't have, taking more and more of what little he had to give.

I'm going to die, he felt—or rather *knew*.

The clock followed, impressing into his forehead for all to see, but it ran backward not forward. It was the clock of life and every heartbeat meant another second gone. Another moment lost and soon he would be no more.

In front of him, a pedestrian hopped in the back of a long, jeep-like vehicle with chrome sides and mud flaps that said, *God Saves*. A *jeepney*, he recalled—the public transportation of the Philippines. The clock still followed, so he jumped in behind the woman and sat quickly. When the vehicle started moving, he looked out the back, didn't see the clock. Perhaps it didn't see him.

He scrunched his head low; they were staring, more dark eyes turned his way. Two young boys gaped at him. *My God, what must I look like? What has happened to me?*

Someone nudged his arm and pointed forward. The driver glanced back, holding out his hand. Charlie reached into his pocket, but it was empty. He'd left the hotel without money. The people stared as the driver called back. They slowed in traffic and out he leaped. Running again, weaving between cars, then onto the sidewalk. His lungs burned, eyes streaming. The darkness chased close behind, the time, the aliens, the Death Angel.

Then a pinnacle towered against the sky with a man below it. A statue, he realized. How he wished it to be the Christ on the cross, his salvation at hand. He ran even though his feet ached, then slowed through the crowds, broke free, jumped the low chain and raced toward the towering statue. From the sides, he spotted the soldiers, heard their shouts as if from a faraway place. He reached the monument and threw himself at the stone base wishing to climb and grab the statue's feet. The sunset shone upon the man's gentle face and on the book resting in his arms.

But Charlie was being pulled away and handcuffed even as he strained to see. Hours might have passed. Somewhere outside himself he knew he'd been brought to a jail, gone through a processing, and now waited in a cell. His knees against his chest, he wondered if the wind was picking up outside—was it afternoon again? Was he still in Manila?

Someone there, he could see their shoes. "We meet in person at last, Charlie."

The voice sounded familiar.

"I saw you on the news just as I was finally venturing from the hotel." It was Maggie. "Instead of testing my faith with food, I came here."

He didn't move.

"You aren't going to speak? Well, I need to tell you. They are sending you home."

"Home?" he whispered, then, "No, they can't. I can't go back." It would kill him for certain. Another trip across that date line, the gall to try reclaiming that lost day. He only knew he couldn't go back now.

"And I'm going to escort you," she said firmly. "This little vacation of mine hasn't gone as planned. Did you know you were clinging to the Rizal Monument? Their national hero in the Philippines."

If only that stone man could truly save him, he thought.

"I talked to your wife. The hotel manager asked me to speak with her."

He looked at her then. "My wife?"

"She left message after message at the hotel. She's worried and said she's sorry. She wants to give it another try after all."

He began to cry. The tears flowed with a depth of pain that surely would split him in two if he didn't stop. But he couldn't stop. The door opened and Maggie was there, her arm around his shoulders.

"I've messed up my whole life. She told me it was over, that time was after me and my life was meaningless. Everything she said is true. I've done nothing. My life is made up of mediocrity and broken promises."

"What are you doing?"

He wiped his face and looked into soft gray eyes. Her question was so simply asked, so non-dramatic.

"You look like death, and yet, aren't you still breathing? Snap out of it." She shook him then, harder than seemed possible for a woman of her age. "So you lost a day, one measly day. You had a bit of a breakdown, nearly lost your wife. You gonna ruin the rest of your days over it? People lose days all the time, but they keep on going. The clock is ticking all right, so quit running around like a maniac and do something."

Wiping his face again, he realized incredulously that it felt like *his* face.

"Yeah, that's right. You look like yourself. It was your own paranoia that got everyone staring at you. I mean, the hat, the ducking around like a criminal. And you do look like that guy from an alien movie. Not the alien but the actor, you silly boy."

"Silly boy?" he repeated. But hadn't he seen something different in the reflection?

He felt tinges of fear as he was released, as they returned to the hotel for his things, and through the entire process of airport security. Could he truly go back, just like that?

Maggie sat beside him on the plane, unfolded his blanket, and plugged in his headphones.

"Will you hold my hand?" he whispered as the wheels left the earth. "Not now, but when it's time. When we cross."

"Of course I will. But why don't you try to sleep."

He did feel the weight upon his eyelids. His delirium of days had included little rest.

"If I die before I wake…" He realized that was part of a childhood prayer.

"You pray the Lord your soul to take," Maggie finished. "Charlie, we should all pray that."

Yes, he did pray the Lord would take his soul once the end came, the coming end, the inevitable destination. A day would be missing from his life. Would that mean redemption of another day?

"Charlie?"

The sound came from far away, like the tinkling of wind chimes in his ears. His eyes opened. "Did I fall asleep?"

"For nearly the entire flight. You're officially back. You lived through it."

"Where are we?"

"Off the U.S. coastline—in the Western Hemisphere."

The wheels of the plane soon touched ground and taxied into the hanger. They de-planed and went through U.S. Customs. He stood close to her the entire time.

Finally, she turned to him. "Goodbye, Charlie. Get back your day and another chance at life all around. We seem assigned to one another, so I'll check on you. And try seeking that God of redemptive days and eternities."

"Thank you, Maggie. I will. Really, I will."

"Next November twenty-third, I'll call, maybe fly out and stay with you and your wife. I'll make sure you're really living."

"Please do. I need the reminder."

So that's exactly what she did.

*   *   *

CINDY MARTINUSEN is the author of six novels including *Winter Passing* and *The Salt Garden*. Her webpage is www.cindymartinusen.com.

Where is Thy Sting?

Nancy Moser

The wind was picking up. It whipped around St. Mark's square in Venice, making Mae Ames pull her sweater close. She bypassed the landmark that drew ordinary tourists and adorned more than its fair share of postcards and guidebooks. St. Mark's Cathedral was everything an eleventh century cathedral should be, yet Mae found it garish. She remembered reading a quote by Mark Twain who'd called it a "warty bug taking a walk." Apt, with all its prickly spires and turrets. The Doges Palace next door didn't interest her, either. Who wanted to see a building where men who had too much power liked to sit around wielding that power?

Boring.

Mae was going to visit a place few tourists saw—and that fact alone pleased her immensely. She was going to the Cimitero di San Michele—the cemetery at San Michele island. Speaking of men with too much power…when good ol' Napoleon had been strutting his stuff, he'd declared there would be no more burying of the dead in Venice with its problematic sea level and lack of real estate. All dead would be ferried out to the island of San Michele. People had complied ever since.

But if Mae was going to get there and back in time to have lunch with her hubby, Collier, after his meeting, she had to get going. She stood under an eave and took out her trusty map. Yes, it made her look like a tourist, but since she *was* a tourist…and if her frizz-bomb blonde hair, her Indian-print skirt, and hippie peasant blouse—all on her fifty-something body—didn't scream to the world that she was just visiting, certainly consulting a map wouldn't be giving up any secrets.

She pinpointed the nearby South Zaccaria Jolanda water bus stop and was off. She passed a phalanx of hunky gondoliers in their striped shirts and flat hats who vociferously offered rides in their gondolas. She waved and blew kisses and they seemed appeased by her womanly attention, if not her money. Now *that* would have been an interesting way to travel to a cemetery island. Yet even with Mae's penchant for the dramatic, a gondola would be too over the top, too Cleopatra on her barge.

She spotted the bus stop. Happily, the #41 was there. Waiting for *her*, no doubt. She paid her fare, walked up the gangplank and under the canvas roof of the *motoscafo*. She found a place on a bench near a window and they took off on the water. After making a few more stops, they headed north across the lagoon. A long wedge of land awaited on the horizon like a slice of thin roast beef sandwiched between the bread of sky and sea.

At this point there was only one other passenger, an old man who had his head nearly buried in the pot of yellow chrysanthemums sitting on his lap. Obviously, chilly days and cemeteries did not appeal to the masses. She left him alone and opened her guidebook. She was immediately taken aback when she read that the dead at San Michele were only allowed the peace of intern-ment for twelve years. Then—because of the space issue—they were dug up and their bones either put in boxes in mausoleum niches (if one had the money to pay for it) or dumped into a communal ossuary. *Ooh, ick.*

But it got worse. In the old days, bones were taken to another island called Sant'Ariano; a regular bone dumping ground. Mae wondered if people's feet crackled when they walked on that island. She shivered at the thought.

And if they were always digging up people…"What happens to the grave-stones?" She hadn't meant to speak out loud and glanced at the old man, hop-ing she hadn't disturbed him.

She found him staring at her. Not just looking. Staring.

"Sorry," she said, then remembered a phrase she hoped would translate well in this situation. "*Mi scusi.*"

He seemed to accept her apology because his shocked expression changed into one of joy. He beamed at her as if she'd made his day.

She should mis-speak more often.

"Isabella!"

The power behind his voice…

Suddenly, he set the mums on the floor of the boat, moved to her bench, and let off a string of Italian she could not decipher—other than the name Isa-bella, which he repeated.

She scooted away but he angled his body, his knees touching hers. She was nearly pressed against the window now. She looked for help, but whoever was steering this thing wasn't available and was concentrating on the water-road, not a lone old man and a harmless American *turista*.

The old man was close enough for Mae to see the veins in his nose, the chasms of his crow's feet. And his eyes…they were chocolate, deep dark chocolate.

He tried taking her hand, his words continuous and heartfelt. Mae yanked her hand away. "No! Stop it!"

The man stopped his chatter, his face confused. Mae put a hand to her chest. "*Mi nombre es* Mae. Mae Ames." She realized she'd just spoken Spanish, but hoped he'd get the gist of it.

He stared at her in confusion as if she'd said, "I am an artichoke."

Luckily, the pink walls of San Michele loomed close. Within seconds, she would be able to disembark at the church-like docking station. She knew she could outrun him if she needed to. Just get her out of this boat.

The motoscafo slowed, drawing close to the concrete dock. The driver helped her out, and she hurried up the stairs to the elaborate entrance. She looked back and saw the man making his way up the steps. Slower than she, but with determination. The driver disappeared inside the boat, then came out with the man's flowers. He called out, but the man didn't look back. He didn't care about his flowers anymore. His focus was on Mae.

This was not good.

Once through the gate she was tempted to stand her ground, confront him right there, and proclaim, "I am not Isabella. Leave me alone!" but as she saw the wide expanse of graves and tombs, she decided that confrontation might be avoided altogether if she got a head start. Mae scurried through the marble plots, intricate statues, and crosses. Tall cypress trees stood guard all around. She glanced back and saw the man standing at the edge of the cemetery looking after her. He extended a plaintive hand. "Isabella…"

Oh dear. This was bad. Very bad.

She decided she needed the cover of a building, so headed to a chapel nearby. Once inside she pulled up short, an inch away from collision with a monk. "Oh! I'm so sorry. Mi scusi, scusi."

He put a calming hand on her arm. "You all right?"

English! She gestured toward the door and opened it a crack. "The old man thinks I'm someone named Isabella."

"Are you?"

"No. But he's very insistent."

He nodded once. "He must love Isabella very much."

She'd never thought of it that way. And in that instant, the threat softened and reason gained a foothold. He wasn't after Isabella to hurt her, but to love her—which, of course, had its own complications, but was better than the former.

"You be all right?"

She took in a fresh breath. "I'll be fine. *Grazie.*"

He nodded, pointed toward the front of the chapel as if indicating where he'd be if she needed him, then walked away.

Mae stood at the door and studied the old man with different eyes. His shoulders were stooped. From age, sorrow, or both? And he used a cane to walk—toward this chapel where she was hiding as if he were a dangerous stalker.

Enough of this. Maybe it *was* time to talk to him. Maybe she could help him understand that she wasn't his dear Isabella.

Father, help me help him.

But as soon as she'd made the decision not to flee, he stopped abruptly on the path. He looked to the right among the grave markers, then turned and walked amongst them, but slower now, the frenzy in his walk abated.

Mae had to fully open the door to watch his progress, but not once did he look in her direction. His eyes were focused on something else and he soon stopped before a grave that held a white stone cross. He'd obviously remembered the reason he'd taken this trip. Too bad his flowers were back on the dock...

Then the man crumbled to his knees. He raised his face toward heaven and dropped his cane, spreading his hands in supplication.

Mae's heart broke. Before she realized what she was doing, she was on the path, running toward him. He was so consumed with his grief that he didn't notice her approach until she stopped a few feet away. Then his head turned and she saw that his eyes had changed. They were not overflowing with the frenzy or passion of his previous stare. They were awash in sorrow. An arm gestured toward the grave. "Isabella, *mi amor.*"

Mae saw the marking on the gravestone: *Isabella Rosini 1928–1999.* His Isabella. His love.

He fell forward as if his spine could no longer hold his weight, his face cushioned by his hands on the grass. Mae went to him, putting an arm around his shoulders. "Shh. It's okay. Shh." She wished she knew some Italian words of comfort.

He sobbed and let her draw him into her embrace. Instinctively, they rocked. After a few moments, he gathered himself enough to sit on his own. He held up a finger and fumbled as he pulled something from the inside pocket of his suit coat. He offered Mae a picture. "Isabella."

She looked at the photo of a woman with long blonde frizz-bomb hair, a wide face, and a wide smile. She could see the resemblance to herself.

"*Bella, una bellezza.*" He gestured toward the photo, and encompassed Mae with a wave of his hand.

Beautiful. She was honored. "Grazie, Signore Rosini."

He seemed a bit taken aback, then smiled. He put the photo away and attempted to get to his feet. Mae helped him up and he brushed off his knees. She returned his cane and he regained his dignity along with his stance.

They stood there, sharing this awkward moment after sharing one so poignant. He finally pointed at the grave. "Isabella, *morto.*"

Morto. Dead. The word in either language was so stark. So final.

But not final. Suddenly, Mae thought of a word of comfort they could share. She pointed toward the heavens where he'd made his initial plea. "Jesus," she said.

The man's face flooded with peace. He placed a hand to his heart. "*Jesus Christ il mio savior.*"

Even without a translation book, Mae understood. "Jesus is my Savior, too."

He nodded. There was nothing more to say—or that had to be said.

She held out her hand and after a moment's hesitation, he shook it. "*Pace,* Signore Rosini. Peace."

"*Pace...*" He cocked his head and his eyes left the here-and-now for a moment. Then he smiled. "*Pace,* Signora Ames. Peace."

Mae walked away, sincerely glad she'd left the warty bug to the tourists. Then she realized that the gravestones held no more interest to her. She felt a sudden need to be with Collier, to be with the love of *her* life. She'd appreciate him all the more for her experience this morning at the Cimitero San Michele with Signore Rosini. In fact, she had to go to him. Now.

So that's exactly what she did.

*   *   *

NANCY MOSER is the author of eleven novels including *The Seat Beside Me, The Invitation,* and the Christy award winning *Time Lottery.* Mae Ames, the character in her story, is from her Sister Circle series, co-authored with Vonette

Bright. Nancy agrees with the warty-bug description of St. Mark's and also likes to wave at hunky gondoliers whenever the occasion arises. To read more about her books and speaking ministry check out www.nancymoser.com.

Undercover Assignment

Donita K. Paul

The wind was picking up. Teri hung on to the stem of the dandelion with both hands and prayed she would not go flying down Pikes Peak Highway. She preferred controlled flight, thank you very much.

She drew her wings in tight against her back. This kind of wind could do more damage than she wanted to cope with. She had serious business on her mind. With an effort, she got her knees around the stem and started to slip down the slender stalk to safety.

Another gust of wind bent the flower almost to the ground. Teri loosened her grip, hoping to fall with style and land gracefully. Instead the stem popped up straight again and sent her catapulting wildly among the autumn debris.

She landed on an airborne brown oak leaf. It crackled beneath her. A brittle section gave way beneath her knee and her whole leg shot through.

"I hate it when that happens!"

She tried to sit up to get better leverage to pry herself loose from this irregular flying carpet. The shifting of her weight caused the leaf to dip to one side and start a spiraling descent.

"Great! Where's your fairy godmother when you need her?"

Teri stretched out prone across the leaf and tried to correct the dangerous tilt of her aircraft. With her leg piercing the middle of the leaf, her task was impossible. She plummeted with dizzying speed toward a parked black and white vehicle.

Fortunately, she sailed through the open window instead of smashing against the word *police* on the door. Her makeshift glider disintegrated as it impacted a cloth-covered shoulder. She tumbled across an expanse of muscular chest and splatted on the passenger seat.

Teri lay still for a moment, catching her breath. One moment too long. A thumb and index finger pinched her backside. Hoisted into the air, she came face-to-face with a man. A human man. A *big* human man.

She might have been able to pull off her bug imitation if the dog hadn't lunged from the backseat, his paws on the shoulders of the man, and his nose sniffing Teri's featherweight wings.

"Ew! Dog breath!" Teri cringed and put her arms up to ward off a slobbery tongue.

"Down, Crispin!"

The golden retriever obeyed for an instant, then popped up again. This time he remained at a more respectable distance. His chin rested on the man's shoulder. The man tilted his head.

"At first I thought you were a dragonfly."

"I am!" declared Teri.

The man chuckled. "No, you're not."

"I should know what I am, shouldn't I? I am a highly developed species. Ever heard of evolution? I'm at the top of my chain."

"I don't believe in evolution. I believe God created the creatures of the earth. I just didn't know until today that he created fairies."

"Fairy!" Teri shrieked. "You think I'm a fairy? Do you know how ridiculous that sounds?" She tried for a convincing laugh, slightly sardonic, but she'd never done sardonic very well.

The man twisted her from side to side, examining her wings and her clothing, layers of sheer material in the most exquisite colors. Teri had style.

"Hey, you!" said Teri. "You're positively mangling my legs."

"Oh, sorry."

He reached down with his free hand and turned the key in the ignition. Then he had to struggle a bit to reach across his lap to hit the buttons to raise the windows. As soon as all avenues of escape were blocked, he set Teri on the dashboard.

She crossed her legs, fluffed out her skirt, patted her fly-away hair, and shook her shoulders, effectively spreading her wings in a beautiful display. She knew she looked her best with a backdrop of gossamer wings.

From her position on the dashboard, the first thing she noticed was the man's uniform. Literally all of the men of her acquaintance wore tights. Teri couldn't help it. She sighed and batted her eyelashes. A uniform made a man so much more attractive.

The man crossed his arms over his chest. "My name's Clint Baker. Pleased to meet you."

"Teri Tinktinkertink. No Tinkerbell jokes, please. And I haven't decided whether I'm pleased to meet you or not."

He nodded. "It would seem you are in a bit of trouble. What can I do for you?"

"Let me go?"

"Maybe. After I'm convinced you weren't injured by that crash landing and that nothing is chasing you."

She gasped. "How'd you know?"

"I'm a police detective. I've got instincts."

Teri squinted and looked him over. "Ha! I don't believe you. Nothing more than the autumn wind was chasing me. And detectives don't wear uniforms. They wear plain clothes. I've seen enough television to know a few things. And that instinct stuff is from an old movie or something."

Clint Baker chuckled. "Well, I *am* a detective. Right now I'm undercover as a patrolman, trying to catch a man for bribery. As for the instinct, it doesn't take much to know you were blown off course by something other than a strong wind."

Teri uncrossed her legs and re-crossed them with the other leg on top. "You're right, actually." She shrugged and then wiggled her shoulders to perk up her wings. "Normally I don't go out in the wind. None of us do." She squinted and glowered at some unseen opponent. "But Estie Emtallyhoot 'borrowed' my family's feast platter."

"Ah." Clint nodded. "A job for the police."

Teri shook her head. "No need for that. Estie's not a bad fairy, just prone to take what she wants without thinking it through. It's a common failing among my people."

"You're all thieves?"

Teri shot him an unpleasant glare and then composed her features in a gracious smile. "Let's get back to my being blown off course, shall we? I hopped a ride on a Rocky Mountain Magpie since I didn't want to chance flying on my own. The stupid bird stopped for a snack—a bag of chips abandoned under that picnic table over there." She waved a hand to indicate a table in the park's campground. "I'll have you know I sat for a long time, waiting patiently, being tolerant of a less intelligent being."

She huffed, blowing out of her pouting lips a stream of air that went up her face and fluttered her bangs. Her wings quivered, shimmering with iridescent colors in the late afternoon light.

"But enough is enough," she continued. "That glutton was going to finish off every crumb. I stood and stamped my foot. You might not know this, but to remain grounded, a fairy must keep both feet on some surface."

"I didn't know that." Clint responded, his eyes trained on something outside of the car.

Annoyed, Teri got to her feet and turned to peer out the windshield. She followed the man's line of sight to see what could be more fascinating than a captured fairy.

Next to a van in the parking lot, two men stood talking. Clint flipped open the compartment between the two seats and twisted a few knobs. Static came from a little black box. He tapped it with his finger, twisted the knobs again, and slammed the lid shut.

"Blast and double blast!"

"Something wrong?" asked Teri.

"I'm not picking up the transmission. Must be a wire loose somewhere."

Teri preened, smoothing out her dark sleeve and fluffing her colorful skirt. "I could help."

"How?" asked Clint, his eyes never leaving his target.

"I know a bit about electronics."

"Right." Clint was good at sounding sardonic.

"So you think fairies don't do anything but lie around on flowers?

"I haven't thought much about what fairies do since the last time I watched Peter Pan."

"Oh well, I won't hold it against you. We do try to keep a low profile."

He leaned forward, his arms crossed against the steering wheel. "I'm going to miss my cue from Donald."

"Tell me what the cue is and I'll go over there and signal you when he says it. Or I could fix the connection in the transmitter."

"You just want out. Once out, you'd be gone."

"And miss my chance to play heroine?"

Clint looked at her for a moment. "My instinct says to give you a chance. But we know what you think of my instincts."

"Hey, a girl can be wrong. Maybe you do have instincts."

"Well, I have no intention of keeping you, so there's no harm in letting you go."

"You weren't going to keep me?"

"You can't be the first fairy ever snagged. I figure your kind are pretty slippery. So, no point in making grand schemes for what I'm going to do with you. Besides, I believe in keeping domestic animals as pets, not wild."

"Animal! Pet! Wild!" Teri quivered so hard she floated off the dashboard. She raised a fist and shook it at the man. "Clint Baker, you need an education."

"Yeah, right. Meanwhile our chance to nab Hanover is fading quick."

Teri floated down to the dashboard and looked again at the two men.

"Okay, what's the cue?"

"'That's not enough money.'"

"And where's the bug?"

"Behind the rearview mirror."

Teri looked over the situation. The men stood next to the front door on the driver's side of the van. "Right at their shoulders. I'll do my dragonfly imitation. They'll never see me."

"The wind has died down some, but not enough. How are you going to get over there?"

"Crispin."

The dog whined.

Teri flew off the dashboard and landed on the dog's neck, taking hold of his collar.

Clint twisted to see his dog with a fairy behind his collar. She looked a bit like a gladiator, but maybe not as fierce. "If you can't get the wire connected, how are you going to signal me? I doubt I can see you at that distance."

"Crispin will chase his tail."

Clint frowned at the two men on the other side of the parking lot. "He never chases his tail."

Teri rolled her eyes. "Puh-lease!"

"Okay, okay."

"Open the back door," Teri ordered, a grin of pure mischief on her tiny features.

Clint reached back for the door handle. "You be careful. The tall guy would just a soon kill you as squash a bug."

"Was that supposed to be funny?"

"There's not an ounce of humor in this reality." Clint still had his hand on the handle, but hadn't pulled. "Hanover is arranging to bribe a police officer, that's me. He transports illegal aliens, and he doesn't treat them like family while doing it."

"Okay, I'll be careful. Let us out."

Clint pulled on the handle and the door swung open. Crispin whined. "It's all right, boy. Go with the little lady."

The dog hopped out of the car, circled the area, sniffing and marking a few spots, then ambled over to the car. He examined the front tire of the van. Clint watched a blur rise up off the dog and fly to the large rectangular mirror.

"Blast! Can't see what she's doing." He reached in the glove compartment and pulled out binoculars.

Checking to make sure the men's attention was on each other and not him, he raised the binoculars and focused on the mirror beside them. He saw a dragonfly darting from one side of the mirror to the other, hovering, darting, hovering again. Then it landed on the chrome bar holding the mirror away from the door.

He could see Teri now. She reached on tiptoe to a black line dangling over her head.

"Keep both feet planted on that bar, little girl," Clint muttered between clenched teeth.

The target moved suddenly, slapping the hood of the car. Clint dropped the binoculars into his lap just as the tall man turned and gestured to the parked police car.

Clint heard a scritching noise from the box between the seats. He opened the console and twisted a knob.

Hanover's voice came through loud and clear. "How many times you gonna say that's not enough money? I'm not in business to give you all my profits."

Clint opened his door to join his partner and make the arrest when the thug planted a fist in Donald's middle. As Donald doubled over, Hanover kneed him in the face and shoved him to the side. In a flash, Hanover flung open the door of the van, slammed it shut, and took off.

Clint pulled his own door shut, twisted the key in the ignition, flipped the siren switch, and took off after him. With one hand on the steering wheel, he turned onto Pikes Peak Highway and skidded across the dirt road. With the other hand he flipped on his radio. He barked out his position and alerted the roadblock at the bottom of the mountain that the suspect was headed their way.

The chase down the mountain sent adrenaline through Clint's system even though he only had to keep the man in sight, not stop him. The roadblock would do that.

The van zigzagged erratically. Even at that speed, the driver should have been able to keep to the road. The van swerved once again, fishtailed, and spun out. A stand of pines kept the vehicle from plummeting over a sheer drop.

Clint stopped and sprinted across the road. He pulled the man out of the van and threw him face forward against the hood. With typical police efficiency, he had the man spread-eagled, cuffed, and listening to his rights in short order.

Hanover cursed and squirmed.

"Hold still," barked Clint.

Hanover cursed again. "Dragonfly! Stupid dragonfly kept flying in my face."

Clint laughed out loud. "Man, if you only knew."

"What do you mean?" growled his prisoner.

Clint shook his head. "I don't think there's any harm in telling you. That wasn't a dragonfly. That was an undercover fairy."

Another stream of profanities poured out of the cuffed man's mouth.

"Hey, watch your language. There may be a lady present." Clint looked around, hoping to see Teri. She was nowhere in sight.

Forty-five minutes later, Donald and Crispin had been picked up and brought down. Another police car hauled the villain away.

Clint, ready to do the interminable paperwork and call it a day, got back into his patrol car. He grinned when he saw Teri standing on his dashboard, poised as an ornament.

"Will you jiggle when we go over bumps?"

"Just like one of those hula dancers," she answered.

"Aren't you going to go after Estie and retrieve your family's feast platter?"

"I have a dozen sisters who'll take care of that. I wanted the glory of being the first to catch up to her."

"So what are you going to do?"

She shrugged, rippling her wings. "I kind of like being an undercover fairy."

Clint laughed. He reached back his hand to stroke Crispin's silky ears. "What do you say, boy?"

The dog whined.

"Right. Miss Teri, would you consider joining our team?"

So that's exactly what she did.

*   *   *

DONITA K. PAUL has written award-winning Christian romance and has now ventured into fantasy. Her latest books *Dragonspell* and *DragonQuest* are allegories that have found fans among old and young. Mother, teacher, and now grandmother, Ms. Paul has been telling stories for over forty years. Check out her personal website at www.donitakpaul.com and explore www.dragonspell.us to learn more about her amazing cast of characters in the fantastic world of Amara.

The Best Laid Plans

Gayle Roper

The wind was picking up. Allie Jamison held the hood of her raincoat snug about her head as she raced for the Visitors' Center at Glen Canyon Dam in northern Arizona, the bill of her baseball cap protecting her face. She pushed through the door and turned to her friend Susan, only to find she wasn't there. Allie looked back toward the parking lot, but Susan wasn't anywhere in sight. She was undoubtedly still in the car, pouting.

Allie sighed. Susan was proving to be a great disappointment.

"We should have gone on a cruise like I wanted," Susan said at least ten times every day for the week they'd been vacationing. She looked at the Grand Canyon and said, "Pretty big hole. I'm going back to the lodge and sun bathe." She looked at the magnificent monoliths of Monument Valley and said, "I like sand beaches better."

Allie sighed. She had had such high hopes for this vacation. She'd managed to slip away without anyone in the media being aware. For once she was going to be a regular person doing regular things. No glamour. No glitz. No paparazzi. In fact, if anything, it was dirt and sweat as she hiked in the Grand Canyon and took glorious photos of the Valley at sunset.

"Can't you just see John Wayne riding after the bad guys?" she'd asked Susan just last night as the lowering sun painted the rocks golden.

"Who's John Wayne?" Susan asked without much interest.

Maybe she should just send Susan on that cruise and continue alone. She'd obviously asked too much of a friendship built on sitting next to each other in a UCLA English class. And trying to talk about Jesus with Susan was a true effort in futility.

"I'm sure Jesus is fine for you," Susan said, "but I don't need Him. I mean, I've got God and She likes me just the way I am."

Such heresy all but stole Allie's breath. So did Susan's refusal to enjoy the trip. She took today's rain as a personal slight and a plot against her happiness.

"Where's your friend, Allison James?" a grating voice asked Allie from way too close for comfort.

Allison James. He knew who she was, knew her stage name.

"Allie Jamison," she corrected, trying not to show her distaste and distress as she aimed a vague smile over the shoulder of slimy Kip Whatever. She couldn't remember his last name, probably because she hadn't listened when he said it because she didn't want to know it. Somehow he kept popping up everywhere she and Susan went.

He had been at the Grand Canyon when they were there, often on the same ranger-led hikes or eating at the same restaurant. He'd stopped last evening to be sure they weren't having car trouble when Allie was waiting for the right lighting for her photos. At least his presence then had stopped Susan's whining for a few minutes. Now here he was at the dam at the exact same time she was. A reporter? A fan? Or a stalker? Whichever, his phobic interest made her uneasy.

As the tour group minus Susan followed the guide down into the bowels of the dam, Allie did her best to stay away from Kip. Why couldn't it be the tall blond guy near the back of the group or his equally handsome dark-haired friend who showed such an interest in her? Of course she didn't look much like herself with her duck shoes, ratty jeans, dripping coat and LA Lakers cap, her red-gold hair pulled through the back in a slapdash ponytail. In fact no makeup had touched her face for the whole week, much to Susan's disgust.

Allie's skin prickled as she became aware of Kip creeping up on her again. Turning abruptly, she worked her way to the back of the group and sidled up next to the tall, blond guy.

"My name's Allie, and that guy over there is bothering me. Can I hang with you two for the rest of the tour?"

The blond raised an eyebrow in surprise, but he smiled and said, "Sure. I'm Trevor and this is Jase. We left our shining armor at home, but we'll do our best to protect you."

"Stand here between us, pretty Allie," Jase said with a look in Kip's direction that stopped him in his tracks.

"Thank you!" She stepped into the safety of their size and kindness. "I was starting to feel like Marian in *The Music Man*. You know, where she tells her mother about not allowing a common masher near her because she has her standards where men are concerned."

Both men looked at her without the vaguest sign of understanding her reference. Didn't anyone today like the old movies or listen to the old musical soundtracks?

"Got it!" Jase snapped his fingers and pointed at her. "*The President's Daughter*, right?"

Allie brought her finger to her lips in a mute plea for silence. She had so hoped no one would recognize her. She looked completely different from the pampered, beautiful girl who appeared in millions of homes each Tuesday night.

Jase nodded. "My lips are sealed."

"The President's daughter?" Trevor blinked. "Wow! Really? Where's the Secret Service?"

"I left them at home. That's why I need you. And please be quiet. I'm traveling incognito."

When the tour was over, Allie thanked her rescuers and headed for the door, hoping to get the jump on Kip. She stopped so abruptly that Trevor walked into her.

"What's wrong?" he asked, looking around.

Allie pointed to the pile of belongings resting beside the door, a beige folder lying on top. "That's my stuff. What's it doing here?"

On the beige folder Susan had written, "I'm out of here. Big mistake on my part. Your Jeep will be in your driveway. You can rent a car in Page."

No signature. No apology. No friend.

"Just like that she left you?" Trevor was a mix of sympathy and disbelief. "And took your car?"

"At least she doesn't plan to keep it." *And I can afford to rent one. She can't.*

Allie quickly leafed through the neat folder Benelli Travel had given her. Everything she needed was there. *Thank you, Susan.*

Still she felt like crying. What more could go wrong on her great adventure? She had prayed so long and so hard about this two-week trip, and she'd been certain that it would be her opportunity to show Susan what being a Christian was all about. Well, that plan had just fallen as flat as the pilot she'd shot three years ago about a college co-ed who wasn't into sex. She sighed. Maybe she should just take Susan's abandonment as a sign from the Lord to go home. "So how do I get to Page to get a car?"

"We can take you," Trevor said. "We're driving through there on our way to Moab and Arches National Park."

"That's where we were going." Allie held out her Benelli folder. "Three nights on a dude ranch just outside Moab."

"Then ride all the way with us," Trevor said.

Every horror story Allie'd ever heard about riding with strangers leapt to her mind and made her hesitate. Then she looked out the door and saw Kip skulking behind the Glen Canyon Dam sign. The rain may have stopped, but his unhealthy attention hadn't.

Trevor and Jase had to be better than risking Kip.

"Only thing is—" Trevor began.

Uh-oh. Here it comes.

"—we're going on a raft ride down the river first." Trevor pointed down Glen Canyon.

"White water?" Allie asked, uncertain. At the Grand Canyon she'd learned all about the death-defying journey of Major John Wesley Powell, a one armed survivor of the Civil War who with ten men shot the rapids of the Green River and the Colorado River down through the Grand Canyon in the late 1800's.

"Wish it were white water," Trevor said, "but it's a float trip. And we stop to see Indian petroglyphs along the way."

So, after a bus ride down a dark tunnel burrowed into the very sides of the canyon, Allie found herself in a fat raft at the foot of the dam, preparing to float down the Colorado River. The last to climb aboard was Kip, who had managed to follow her yet again.

"Wow! What a great idea this is," he said, looking in Allie's direction. She became very interested in the clips on her life jacket.

Everyone wore yellow slickers provided by the rafting concession. When it began to rain again, like magic little waterfalls appeared all over the walls of the canyon.

Watching the lovely sight, Allie leaned against a fat side with Trevor beside her. She closed her eyes. "God is good."

"All the time," Trevor returned softly.

Allie's eyes flew open and she sat up, embarrassed. "I didn't realize I said that out loud."

"I just spent many months saying that very thing as I spit sand out of my mouth or prayed my way through a patrol or—" He made a half smile. "But you don't want to hear my war stories in the middle of this beauty."

Allie had opened her mouth to contradict him when the guide directed the raft to shore. Everyone climbed out for a hike to see the petroglyphs. Allie noticed Kip trailing her constantly, but he didn't get too close. When they climbed back into the rafts, he moved as near as he apparently dared, given her escort.

"I wouldn't worry about him," Trevor said. "He doesn't look like an enemy agent to me—unless the enemy's in worse shape than I thought."

Allie smiled at Trevor's little joke. "I'm more worried about a stalker or the paparazzi."

Trevor turned to her, and his brow furrowed. In fact, to her surprise, he suddenly looked angry. "Or kidnappers," he said. "It just dawned on me that you are a risk to national security wandering around by yourself."

"Me?"

"Believe me," he continued, "I wasn't fighting so you could get kidnapped and be held for ransom by some terrorist cell."

"What?"

Jase, who was sitting in front of Allie and Trevor, turned. "He thinks you're really the President's daughter. Remember, he's been out of the country."

Allie was distracted by a pre-teen girl climbing to her in the raft. "Aren't you *The President's Daughter*?"

Allie nodded.

"Wow!" the girl said. "None of my friends will believe this! Can I have my picture taken with you? Hey, Mom, I was right. It *is* Allison James."

Forcing a smile, Allie looked at the girl's mother while the woman snapped three pictures.

"I bet the real Secret Service wouldn't let that happen," she muttered, miffed that her identity was blown. She could feel the others in the raft looking at her.

"God is good," Trevor said. "But you've got me thoroughly confused. Are you or are you not the President's daughter?" He turned to Jase. "One of them is blonde, isn't she?"

"All the time," Allie replied and knew she had to jettison her bad attitude, not only over Kip and over the pictures, but also over the fact that her wonderful, prayed-over plans had bombed. After all, what trouble had it been to make a kid happy? So Susan split, stranding her. She could manage. What if Kip was a bit scary? God was still good. He was still in charge of the universe and of her life, even if neither seemed to go the way she wanted. That was what faith was all about, wasn't it? Accepting God's goodness even when He seemed more mysterious than ever?

"I play the President's daughter in a TV show called *The President's Daughter*." Allie smiled at Trevor. "I would never cause an international incident even if someone cared enough to kidnap me, though if someone did, God would still be good, wouldn't He?"

"All the time," Trevor said as the raft pulled into Lee's Ferry and the trip ended.

Allie climbed into the front seat of Jase's truck and prayed her way to Moab, Utah, a rental car, and the dude ranch. When the evening passed without a Kip sighting, she began to relax. God was good.

"Isn't this a great place, Allison?" Kip greeted her the next morning in the dining room. He gave her what he probably thought was an endearing smile.

Allie shuddered. Enough was enough. "Kip, leave me alone! If you don't, I'm calling the police."

Kip's mouth dropped open. Then he turned and walked away, shoulders hunched.

Allie stared at her breakfast, appetite gone. *I certainly handled that well, didn't I?*

A few minutes later Kip re-entered the dining room and took a seat as far from Allie as possible. She tried to ignore him by studying her Benelli Travel folder until Trevor and Jase arrived to take her on a Jeep trip into Canyonlands.

"Too bad we didn't know about this ranch," Trevor said as he ate her toast for her. "It's great."

Allie smiled for the first time since she'd seen Kip. "Benelli Travel." She tapped her folder.

"Look, Larry," a lady two tables over said in a carrying voice. "It's—"

Oh, no! Not again! Allie turned her face away.

"—Kip Benelli! Thanks, Kip! Great trip!"

Benelli! Allie spun toward Kip who was shaking hands with the woman and Larry. She rose and wove between tables toward him, Trevor and Jase following. Was she more angry or embarrassed? She wasn't sure. She thrust her packet at him.

"You're Benelli Travel?"

Kip nodded.

"Why don't I know you?"

"You worked with one of my agents, Mary Alice, not me."

"Oh. Of course. Well, are you following me or not?"

Kip looked uncomfortable. "Yes, sort of."

"Yes?" Anger won.

"But no, not like you think."

"Yes or no?" she demanded.

"I just wanted to be certain you had a wonderful time."

"Do you often follow clients?"

"No, but clients aren't usually TV stars who can help make or break a company."

"I bet he wants you to make an ad about how wonderful the trip was, thanks to Benelli Travel," Trevor said.

Kip's already red face flushed scarlet.

Jase barked a laugh. "He does!"

"I did," Kip said. "But no more. I'm sorry I scared you, Allison. I never meant to."

"Allie. I thought you were a reporter or a stalker."

He nodded. "Don't worry. I'm going home this morning. I won't bother you again."

Allie studied him a minute. "Were you planning on the Jeep tour of Canyonlands today?"

He nodded. "But not any more."

"Sure you are," she said. "You're coming with us." She indicated herself, Trevor and Jase.

Kip looked at her with hope in his eyes. "But I want you to have a good time."

So that's exactly what she did.

*   *   *

GAYLE ROPER is the award winning author of thirty-nine books. She has been a Christy finalist, has won the Romance Writers of America's RITA Award for Best Inspirational Romance, the Holt Medallion, the Inspirational Readers Choice Book of the Year, the Reviewers Choice Award, and the Lifetime Achievement Award. She speaks at women's events and writers' conferences across the nation and is a staff member of CLASS. She lives with her husband Chuck in southeastern Pennsylvania where they enjoy their family of two great sons, two lovely daughters-in-law, and the world's five greatest grandkids. Gayle enjoys reading, gardening, and eating out every time she can talk Chuck into it.

Cyberspace Savior

Jefferson Scott

The wind was picking up. Or so it seemed. Palms swayed gently in the virtual breeze. Simulated waves washed upon silicon sand, cut by Higgins' landing craft and the Japanese battleship *Hiei*. Overhead, Zeroes tangled with Corsairs, while "Val" dive bombers rained 500-pound death on U.S. troops diving for the dubious cover of the bamboo huts of Guadalcanal.

MoG=Heb=NarrowRoad laid his last landmine just this side of the ridge Japanese tanks would be most likely to approach. They would never be able to see the mines—NarrowRoad would protect his flag and rack up his score. He scampered up the ladder of the watchtower to wait for his next victim. An SBD bomber droned overhead on its way to Japanese-held flags elsewhere on the island.

He turned his attention to the red and blue text messages scrolling up the left side of the screen. One player was complaining that his team was made up of sons of questionable parental origin. Another gave orders that the rest of the players were happily ignoring. A third continued his whining that a high-scoring player was using an aimbot or other "hack" to cheat his way to a top score.

Then a gray message appeared on the screen. Gray text was automated announcement text. Server administrators used these to give standing rules or recruitment messages for the clan or club who owned the server. This one said, "Welcome to the Men of God (MoG) server, where Jesus is Lord."

NarrowRoad braced for the reaction that message always got. The few players who weren't busy shooting or being shot would sometimes read the gray text, and when they did they usually had something to say.

"What?" came a red text message from a player named Nightm@re. "This is a Christian server?"

NarrowRoad typed his reply. It appeared as a blue text message on the screen. "That's right. MoG is a Christian clan."

Doing evangelism online was a bit like trying to set up church in a Wild West gold rush town. Here, Christianity was not exactly a felt need. But there was a definite thrill to doing it, and NarrowRoad felt the adrenaline begin to flow.

"Yeah, right," Nightm@re replied in red text.

"No, it really is," NarrowRoad typed. "We're all Christians who love gaming. Glad you're playing on our server today."

"So," Nightm@re wrote, "amen and pass the ammo? Christians killing each other in a wargame. Typical hypocrisy."

Just then a Japanese scout slipped down the hillside and hid at the base of the flag NarrowRoad was protecting. The guy hadn't seen him in the watchtower. NarrowRoad pulled out his TNT packs and dropped one over the edge. A swift plunge of the detonator—*BOOM*—a flying Japanese body, and back to more important matters.

"It's not hypocritical," NarrowRoad wrote. "Jesus was not a pacifist."

"Whatever."

One of NarrowRoad's clan mates who happened to be among the twenty-four players on the server right then, *MoG*=Jer=SavedOne entered the conversation. "ya. remember he turn ovr those tables @ the temple?" Online, the emphasis in spelling was on brevity, not grammatical correctness.

A player by the name of [SoMF]+Ownage chimed in. "Shut up and play the game."

"Christians are losers," said eatmyshorts.

NarrowRoad smiled to himself. "Hey, Nightm@re, you're right about one thing. Christians are hypocrites. Me included. But guess what? So are you."

"Are you stoned?"

"No, just listen. A hypocrite is someone who says he believes something, but doesn't actually live it out, right?"

"No," Ownage wrote, "a hypocrite is a Christian with a Rolls Royce."

"hey," SavedOne wrote, responding to the earlier message (not everyone typed as quickly as NarrowRoad), "this a Christian srvr. we talk about jesus, ok? u can go 2 somepl8ce else if u want."

NarrowRoad continued typing. "But you're a hypocrite, Nightm@re, because you say one thing but don't always live it. Like let's you say you tell your mother you always go the speed limit, but lots of times you don't. That's being a hypocrite."

The whiner typed a message. "Nice score, cheater! Everybody, DucksFan is a haxor."

"Not me," Nightm@re wrote. "I say I DON'T obey the speed limit, so am I a hypocrite when I slow down?"

"Exactly."

"Way to blow me up, moron," Ownage typed. "I swear you guys are all noobs."

"nightmare," typed SavedOne, "r u chad?"

"What?"

"r u chad? r u brian's friend from u.t. austin?"

"Uh...no. Sorry. Wrong guy."

"k. his name is nightmare, 2."

The turret of a Japanese tank appeared atop the ridge below NarrowRoad. He watched with relish. The tank sped over the crest, zooming to capture the supposedly unguarded flag.

BOOM.

The tank turned into charcoal and rolled over, flaming. The kill message flashed on the screen: "133tONE killed [landmine] by *MoG*=Heb=Narrow-Road."

That is so choice, NarrowRoad thought. The only problem now was that his line of mines had a gap in it. He shimmied down the ladder, grabbed new mines from the ammo box, and headed for the ridge.

Bullets flew around him from somewhere. He zigged and zagged toward the ridge. Just across, he could hear another vehicle approaching. His health bar took a hit. Who was shooting at him? He dropped the new landmines, his health bar shrinking steadily, and turned back toward his watchtower.

There sat a Japanese light tank, its machine gun spitting at him.

I knew I should've mined all approaches! This was his final thought as his health bar disappeared and the game generated his death wheeze sound effect.

MoG=Heb=NarrowRoad killed [Chi-Ha] by {{101st}}FURY.

He clicked Respawn, but knew his flag would be captured before the game would let him rejoin the action. In ten seconds his mines would disappear. Such was life and death in *Battlefield 1942.*

As he waited to respawn, he cycled up through the text messages he had missed while he'd been dodging bullets. Nightm@re had asked him a question and then followed up with a few "You there, Narrow?" messages. The question: "You really believe this Jesus stuff?"

Dear Lord, NarrowRoad prayed, *guide my words.*

"Hey, Nightm@re," he typed. "You still there?"

"Narrow! Thought you'd left."

"Nah, just had to focus on the game for a sec. Got your text."

A message came through from the whiner. "DucksFan and Ownage use hacks."

"Shut up," someone wrote.

"Am not," DucksFan typed.

"4get it," eatmyshorts said. "bad playas always say good playas use hacks."

"Nightm@re," NarrowRoad typed, "I do believe all the Jesus stuff. Built my whole life on it, man. You wanna talk about it?"

The game respawned NarrowRoad at the rear American base, beside three parked Sherman tanks. He got in one and drove toward his favorite flag, which was now flying Japan's colors. Let the rest of the players fight for the other three flags. This one was *his.*

"Sure," Nightm@re typed. "I guess. You're like the third person to bring it up to me in like two weeks. Weird."

"Okay," NarrowRoad said. "I'll stop playing and we can talk." He pulled the tank off the road to concentrate on his typing. "You wanna leave the game and talk privately? You have MS Messenger?"

"Nope."

"What about ICQ?"

"What's that?"

"Okay," NarrowRoad wrote, "never mind. We'll do it here."

"Ya."

"The first question I have is whether or not you're a Christian. Are you?"

"I don't think so."

"Hey, lovebirds," the whiner wrote. "Get a room."

"ya," Fury wrote, "shut up and play the @#$% game."

Another gray message: "Check out our forums: www.menofgod.us/bf."

"Then that's where we'll start," NarrowRoad typed.

"Where are you?" Nightm@re answered.

"By the American base. You gonna bomb me?"

"LOL. No. Let's meet."

"hey," came SavedOne's belated reply, "no cussing on this srvr. pls keep it clean. fam friendly. k?"

"Meet me on the W beach."

NarrowRoad smiled. "Affirmative. Be there in a sec."

He turned the tank west and took the cliff-side road along the edge of the island. Out in the ocean he saw a periscope cutting through the water. Fun was being had by all.

Then he heard an ominous sound he knew too well—a sound one didn't often live through: a Val bomber diving right for him. The whistle of the bombs. All he could do was cringe.

WH-TOOM!

The tank's health bar dropped to nothing and forward progress stopped. Flame crackled in his speakers. He jumped out and dove toward the ocean's edge—just as the tank exploded, taking a massive chunk out of NarrowRoad's own health bar.

But when he hit the ground, he wasn't dead. The Val banked sharply to come back and finish the job. But a Corsair zoomed between the hills and sliced it apart in midair. The Corsair wagged its wings and banked back toward the main battle.

NarrowRoad typed, "Thank you, pilot!" and headed on to the beach.

He crested a hill and saw his sworn enemy—a Japanese assault trooper—standing there, automatic rifle pointed right at him.

"Nightm@re?" he typed. "That you?"

The Japanese figure hopped up and down. "Ya."

NarrowRoad chuckled. "No weapons, k? I'm almost dead as it is."

"Sure." Nightm@re put away his rifle and pulled out a grenade. It made him look mostly unarmed.

NarrowRoad moved in front of him. There they stood, face to face, eye to eye, supposed enemies—different uniforms and, at the moment, different eternal destinies—with fighters dogfighting overhead and sounds of the *Hiei* shelling the island from somewhere in the distance, on the beaches of one of the most storied islands of the second world war. Speaking about eternity. The image lodged in NarrowRoad's mind with singular clarity.

"All right," he typed, "let's go at it like this. God is holy—perfectly pure—and can't have anything not pure around Him. But in the Garden of Eden, Adam and Eve disobeyed God. This made them impure, so God had to cast them away from Him. But God has always wanted to have man near Him. So He came up with a plan."

Over the course of their conversation, the bombs continued to fall. A "helpful" teammate came and shoved a bayonet through Nightm@re's ribs (he respawned and made it back to the beach). An SBD pilot chased them around the beach with three wavetop passes, trying to clip them with his wings. A few

Men of God members chimed in to help NarrowRoad's explanation. Lots of players complained—they saw the whole conversation on their screens, too, a fact that pleased NarrowRoad. There was even a technical hiccup that booted everyone from the server and restarted the game on the same map.

But in the end, nothing could keep Nightm@re—or, more accurately, the human being behind the name, who happened to be a young Brit named Dean—from coming to faith in the Lord Jesus Christ.

As they concluded a discussion of what to do next, NarrowRoad looked out to sea, where a Japanese battleship was steaming into view. The whiner's name hovered in the air over the ship, indicating he was the one driving it.

"Looks like our friend wants to shut us up once and for all," NarrowRoad said.

The ship's main turrets rotated toward the beach.

"Ya," Nightm@re said. "I think she's going to open up with all guns."

"Well, it's been great, my friend," NarrowRoad typed. "Remember what I said about finding a good church, okay?"

"Sure will. Thanks so much, mate."

"No problem at all, bro," NarrowRoad wrote. "This is exactly why we're here."

The first salvo from the battleship flattened the beach and the hillside just beyond where they were standing. The impact of the shells shook their speakers. Their health bars took a serious dip.

"Die, Christians!" the whiner typed.

The battleship looked like she was going to drive right up onto the beach to silence their talk.

And that's exactly what she did.

∗   ∗   ∗

JEFFERSON SCOTT writes technothrillers and military suspense novels. His Ethan Hamilton novels feature a virtual reality programmer caught up in high-tech action, and his *Operation: Firebrand* military thrillers center around a covert ops team on missions of mercy in the world's hotspots. Scott's non-fiction includes *Be Intolerant,* with Ryan Dobson, and *Say Goodbye to Stubborn Sin,* with Clark Gerhart. He and his family live in Orlando, Florida. Visit Jefferson Scott online at <u>www.jeffersonscott.com</u>.

The Rescuers

Robert Whitlow

The wind was picking up.

Nova couldn't feel it, but she could hear it in the tops of the trees. Wrapped in a gray cloak that melded into the tree's rough bark, she looked up as a stronger gust of wind caused the leaves overhead to stand out like a thousand tiny green banners signaling the advance of an invisible army. There was an army out there. It was looking for her.

She put her head down and closed her eyes. She hadn't moved in over five hours. She heard a rustling along the ground. She peeked around the edge of the tree. A camouflaged form crept across the ground toward her.

"Vera!" she hissed. "You weren't supposed to move until I gave the signal."

The figure raised her head and Nova saw her younger sister's dark brown eyes and mud-stained cheeks.

"I'm scared!"

"That's no excuse! Get down!"

Vera collapsed on the ground and didn't move. Nova waited, refusing to give in to the impulse to beckon her sister closer. Lack of discipline was not an option. Perfect obedience to commands was the only hope of survival.

Silence returned to the forest as the sisters waited for the sun to creep below the edge of the horizon. As the last rays dimmed, Nova allowed herself to breathe more freely. In one of the great paradoxes at the end of the age, darkness had taken over the light, but light still reigned in the darkness.

She heard rustling on the other side of her tree. She whirled around, her eyes not fully adjusted to the shadows, but every other sense at highest alert. Before she could react it was upon her.

She grappled with it as she fell backward. Experienced by years of warfare, she sensed its considerable strength. Yielding slightly, she used the leverage created by momentary weakness to shift to a hold designed to gain the precious seconds needed for survival. The creature's stale breath, laced with paralyzing poison, wrapped around her head. It pushed her hard against the ground as its fangs sought to inject their poison directly into her left ear. Through the haze, she saw into the second realm. The creature had been a computer programmer in San Jose before the darkness took him.

"I know your name," Nova said through clenched teeth. "You are Harvey Donnally."

The creature only grunted, but Nova felt its grip weaken. It drew back its head. The shadows lengthened. Nova's power increased.

"You've been following me for three days," she continued. "My sister and I knew you were there, but now I know your name. Where are the others?"

The haze lessened, but she maintained her hold on the creature and thus her window into the second realm. She saw the other members of the patrol. There were fourteen in all. Not as many as she feared. Probably only a scouting party. The creature served as second in command.

"Harvey, I know you can hear me," she said, her voice growing softer.

The creature released its hold on her, but Nova maintained a tight grip on him.

"What about your masters?" she demanded. "What are their coordinates?"

Nova felt the creature's fear. Even secondhand, the emotion brought a slightly bitter taste to her mouth. Her prisoner struggled to pull away. Vera crept beside her.

"Vera," she said. "This is Harvey Donnally. Do you know how many are in his unit?"

Vera held out her hand and lightly touched the top of the creature's misshapen head. He squirmed under her touch.

"Twelve?"

"Close. There are fourteen. They are about a half mile away in a ravine waiting for daylight. Harvey wasn't supposed to attack by himself, but he couldn't resist trying to be a hero. After all, we are only two females."

"Who know the truth," Vera responded.

Nova smiled. "What else can you see?"

Vera touched the man's head again.

"We should take him in for examination," she said. "He has been near the core."

Nova nodded. "I agree. We've found what we came for."

❧   ❧   ❧

Nova and Vera, each firmly holding one of Harvey's arms, stood with him between them. The sisters locked eyes, and in the power of agreement instantly translated along with their prisoner from the forest floor to the West Coast Hall of Justice. When they landed on the marble floor, Harvey looked around and let out a wail.

"It could be worse," Nova said dryly. "There is a place of judgment beyond this."

"Move along with the prisoner," a burly guard instructed.

"Sorry," Vera said. "We just got here."

They stood before the entrance to the hall. The closer they came to the room, the more energized Nova and Vera felt. Harvey seemed to shrink between the two women. He didn't try to pull away. All fight seemed gone from him. A court official came over to them. No words were exchanged. Unless they chose to do so, men of his rank didn't have to ask questions.

When he left, Vera whispered, "Are we supposed to wait here?"

"Yes, he's going to take us directly to one of the judges."

"Will they use one of the coals—"

"Hush," Nova interrupted, nodding toward Harvey.

The official returned and they followed him into the hall, a high-ceiled room illuminated with light that emanated softly from the walls. There were twelve platforms, one for each judge on duty. The official led them to the left side of the room. The judge, a young man barely older than Vera, sat behind a sky blue bench. Nova looked in his eyes and saw the wisdom of one who had both suffered and believed. He rose as they approached.

"Bring the prisoner here," he commanded.

When they stood before him, the judge reached into a fold of his robe, took out a glowing white rock, and quickly touched it to Harvey's lips. The scream that escaped the man's mouth died before it could crescendo.

"You will now speak the truth," the judge said.

❧   ❧   ❧

After he finished his examination, the judge turned to Nova.

"Is he redeemable?" she asked.

"Only the princes of darkness are beyond hope. Take him to the place of cleansing."

"And us?" Nova asked.

"The information he supplied has already gone to those in authority. You will receive your orders as you leave."

❧   ❧   ❧

As they exited the hall, a military official handed Nova two slips of paper about an inch square.

"Did the coal hurt his lips?" Vera asked in a low voice as they entered a long corridor.

"Only for a second, then it became a balm to the scarring of his soul."

Harvey walked in a more upright position. Nova glanced sideways and could see the two yellow fangs shrinking in size. The sisters delivered him to the white-robed guardians at the entrance to the pools, then relaxed in a refreshing room until the bell rang. Nova stretched and handed one of the tiny squares of paper to Vera.

"Are you ready?" she asked.

"Double-check," Vera replied.

Each woman held a paper up to the light.

"Oops," Nova said. "Do you see why protocol is important?"

"That's why I called for a check."

They exchanged slips. Each placed the correct one in the center of her tongue.

❧   ❧   ❧

They stood at the edge of the surf in the early light of morning. In the distance, rising two hundred feet from the surface of the water, they could see the jagged top of the south tower for the Golden Gate Bridge. The north tower had been destroyed in the first uprising and resulting earthquake. Nova tilted her head to the side in alarm.

"They're coming!" she cried.

"It's out of time!" Vera answered.

The two women left the edge of the water and scrambled up a steep hill of rocky outcroppings that lined the beach. Throwing themselves down behind a large rock they lay still and listened. Nova waited as her cloak adapted to the color of the rock, then, holding it over her head, she looked around the edge toward the water.

There were two riders and twenty warriors on foot. All of them wore helmets. The foot soldiers were sniffing the ground where the two women had landed. She focused on one of the riders. He looked familiar.

It was Caspian.

Nova saw him look up at the rocks. She knew that his eyes, though partially blinded by deception, still retained the capacity to distinguish human forms. The foot soldiers were limited primarily to the sense of smell. Caspian dismounted and began to clamber up the rocks, following the trail the woman had taken. Two ordinary soldiers followed him. The others spread out along the beach.

Nova remained motionless. Details of her orders now made sense. The wind picked up as a storm arose from the sea. As the sea began to surge, the soldiers scampered back and in shrill cries begged Caspian and his companions to come down. Nova willed him closer. She held out her left hand to Vera and with two fingers motioned toward the approaching enemies. Her sister could handle the small ones. Leave Caspian to her. To capture her older brother would be the greatest victory of her life.

Closer they came.

At five feet, Nova launched herself through the air and grabbed her brother by the throat. Vera knocked the two soldiers to the ground and held them motionless. Nova ripped off her brother's helmet and prepared to do battle with his eyes.

It wasn't Caspian!

"Who—" she started.

The creature, empowered by her momentary surprise, thrust aside her hand and dug his fingers into her right shoulder. Nova screamed in pain. At the sound, the others on the beach began to climb as fast as they could up the rocks. Vera struggled, but held the other two soldiers at bay.

"Nova!" Vera called out, "Remember the promise!"

Nova grabbed the creature's other hand as it sought to lodge in her left shoulder. He moved his head toward her mouth, his breath more foul than any she'd ever encountered. She felt faint.

"No weapon formed against me shall prosper," she whispered.

The captain stopped. The clambering troop approached. Nova looked up at the darkening sky.

"No weapon formed against me shall prosper!" she cried out.

Strength entered her and she thrust back her adversary. Whipping the cloak around her shoulders, she jumped onto a nearby rock. Vera released her foes and joined her. The advancing troops hesitated. The two women let their cloaks drop so their faces were in plain view of the two captains.

"Behold!" Nova called. "The faces of the redeemed! You could yet join us before the end comes!"

The captain who had attacked Nova hurled a curse that energized his followers. The women turned and fled up the rocks. The enemies followed for a few feet, but they were no match for the women on uneven terrain. Spewing curses, they stopped. Nova and Vera reached the crest of the hill.

"They'll come around by the easy way," Vera said.

"Which means we'll have to take the harder road to the rendezvous point."

The women began climbing another rock-strewn hill. At the top, they stopped to rest. The sky was clearing. No rain would fall. Their pursuers were far below. The foot soldiers would climb a few feet up the rocks, then return to more level ground. Soon they would tire and look for easier prey.

"You thought it was Caspian, didn't you?" Vera asked.

Nova looked away in shame. "My discernment is not perfect."

Vera's face softened. "I didn't say it to judge you. It speaks of the depth of your love. Your spirit longs to find him and pull him into the light."

Nova felt a tear sting the corner of her eye. She didn't speak. Her brother, her childhood soul mate, had fallen into the enemy's camp. Their parents died hoping for his restoration. Rescuing him was the quest she most wanted to undertake.

Vera stood up straight and a new authority entered her voice. "Now is the time. Part of my present assignment is to commission you. The road will be marked with trials and suffering. It may cost your own life. Do you want this?"

"Yes," Nova answered resolutely.

Vera stepped forward and placed her hands on her sister's head. "Then receive it."

So that's exactly what she did.

∗   ∗   ∗

ROBERT WHITLOW is a practicing attorney and the author of *The List*, *The Trial*, *The Sacrifice*, *Life Support*, and *Life Everlasting*, all published by WestBow Press. For more information please visit his website: www.robertwhitlow.com.

Writing Advice

The Novelists of ChiLibris

Because we are often asked for advice on how to begin or maintain a writing career, we asked our novelists for the most valuable lesson they've learned over the years. What follows is a treasury of rich experience:

The most valuable lesson I've learned about the writer's life is that it is full of ups and downs. In your own eyes, you will never, ever "arrive." Some months you'll be on top and feel wonderful about how things are going, other months you'll be sure your career is over. The sooner you accept that this is normal—and just show up at your desk anyway, day after day after day—the more likely you are to start having more ups than downs. Besides, it's not about you anyway. Though the act of writing may be therapeutic for the writer, a book doesn't really come to life until it's read by someone else. If God uses your story to bring joy or comfort or reproof or wisdom to even one other life, you are a success in the eyes of the only One who matters.
~Deborah Raney, author of *A Nest of Sparrows* (WaterBrook Press).

*   *   *

The most important thing I've learned about writing is to be prepared to fail. I'm not talking about rejections from publishers or magazines; I'm talking about every day on the blank page. I seldom get it right the first time, or the second time, or even the fourth time. But if I give myself permission to NOT be perfect the first time I write a sentence or a paragraph or a chapter, then I show myself a mercy, and also give myself the joy of redeeming what I've written by rewriting it. Writing is a continuous act of creation, and rewriting is a redeeming process—just as we are God's continuing act of creation, and our transformation is a process of redemption. I, as a writer, have learned to give myself room to fail; God as my redeemer, makes something out of that failure.

~Kathryn Mackel, author of *The Departed* (WestBow Press).

*　　*　　*

The most valuable lesson I've learned about writing is that it's about production. Turning out a certain number of words each day, and then polishing those words so they're the best I can do (the polishing comes later, after getting the words out). And as in production of goods, production of words must follow the Japanese principle of *kaizen*—continuous improvement in quality. That means learning the craft and applying what I learn to my words, and doing this over and over again.

~James Scott Bell, author of *Write Great Fiction: Plot & Structure* (Writers Digest Books).

*　　*　　*

The most valuable lesson I've learned about writing is that the old admonition "write your passion" is more than mere mantra—it's essential to developing your calling as a writer. For years I wrote what I thought the market wanted, but then an editor said, "What are *you* dying to write?" That question—and the resulting book—gave me the first glimmer of the writer I was supposed to be when I grew up.

~Angela E. Hunt, author of *Unspoken* (WestBow Press).

*　　*　　*

The most important thing I've learned has been to let myself write badly. Every day I'm still tempted to avoid typing anything that isn't excellent. That just freezes my creativity and I don't get anything written. Instead, I'm training myself to JUST WRITE. Write what's in my heart, what's in my brain, just as it comes out. It looks like a mess, but after that first draft is completed, the real fun begins. As my husband tells me often, "Stop trying to edit the stuff you haven't written yet."

~Janelle Burnham Schneider, author of *British Columbia: The Romantic History of Dawson Creek in Four Complete Novels* (Barbour Publishing).

*   *   *

The most valuable lesson I learned about writing is that it can always be better but sometimes you have to stop and accept that it's as good as it's going to get. If novelists suffered over every line waiting to get it perfect, we'd only write punch lines.

~Nancy Moser, author of *The Seat Beside Me* (Multnomah).

*   *   *

The most valuable lesson I have learned about writing is that it is just like any other job. It's work. I cannot wait to feel inspired or to feel creative. However I feel, I must "do the work." A sense of inspiration or creativity may come after I have written well, which happens just often enough to keep me at the work. As Stephen King says, "this isn't the Ouija board or the spirit-world we're talking here, but just another job like laying pipe or driving long-haul trucks." King advises writers that all they need is a room, a door, and the determination to shut the door until the writing goal for the day is met. It isn't glamorous, but I've learned it's the truth.

~Stephanie Grace Whitson, author of *A Garden in Paris* (Bethany House Publishers).

*   *   *

All through school—through college and then some—I was taught that writing is "recorded thought." I heard this so often that the answer became reflex, like that hinky electric knee-jerk you give when the doctor smacks you with the little rubber tomahawk.

Then one day it dawned on me: writing is not recorded *thought* at all. Writing is recorded *sound*, and the melody the words create can enhance the thought they convey, or it can contradict it, or it can add another dimension that is entirely beyond the tethered confines of subject-verb-predicate. We all have a little person in our head who reads the words to us when we encounter good writing. With *great* writing, the sounds of the words work together, and that little person breaks forth into song.

~Tom Morrisey, author of *Deep Blue* (Zondervan).

*   *   *

Write tight.
~Jane Orcutt, author of *Dear Baby Girl* (Tyndale House).

*   *   *

The most important thing I've learned about writing is that it encompasses a writer's life. A writing career is far more than sitting in front of a computer and creating a story. It's research, editing and digging into the brain to be original and compelling. It's doing revisions, line edits, galley proof edits, and title brainstorming. It's doing interviews, developing a web site, promoting, book signing, and so much more. Yet the rewards are tremendous. My heart sings when I open reader mail to hear that my story has changed someone's life, has moved a person toward the Lord or helped a person see hope in dealing with a life issue. Writing threads through the author's heart and weaves a life-changing fabric.
~Gail Gaymer Martin, author of *Michigan: A Novel* (Barbour Publishing).

*   *   *

The most important lesson I've learned about writing is that you earn the right to say what you want. It's a privilege, not a right, to be published. You pay your dues as in any other business and putting down someone ahead of you will not get to your goal faster.
~Kristin Billerbeck, author of *What A Girl Wants* (WestBow Press).

*   *   *

The most valuable lesson I've learnt is to make friends with other writers. Writing can be an isolating business and, even if you are not particularly extroverted, you need to have people around who understand what it is like to write. You must have someone who can help you to celebrate the joys and share the frustrations. It is essential to have at least one friend who will not assume you are "one chocolate chip short of a cookie" when you talk about the people living inside your head. Networking is important; colleagues in the publishing business are useful, but writing friends are indispensable.
~Penny Culliford, author of *Theodora's Diary* (Zondervan).

*   *   *

What I've learned about writing…God gave me a brain which produces stories; that's the easy bit. The hard bit is getting them to come to life in prose that's easy to read.

~Veronica Heley, author of the Ellie Quicke Mysteries (HarperCollins and Severn House).

*   *   *

The most valuable lesson I've learned about writing is that it's hard work. It's energizing and draining, something I love to do and hate to do, something that's never done, but eventually has to be turned in. I've learned that what's easy to read is hard to write, and what's easy to write is hard to read. I'm a steward of words, and I'm accountable to God for how I arrange them. That's the best reason for working hard at rewriting: "work at it with all your heart, as working for the Lord, not for men" (Colossians 3:23). I need honest critics and careful editors. But above all I need Christ, who said, "Apart from Me, you can do nothing" (John 15:5). When you work this hard at something, you don't want it to amount to nothing. You want it to last forever. You want to hear the Audience of One say, "Well done." No pay-off could be bigger than that!

~Randy Alcorn, author of *Safely Home* (Tyndale).

*   *   *

The most valuable lesson I've learned about writing is to tell the Truth. This sounds like a contradiction, since we novelists apparently get paid for making up all sorts of lies. But don't be misled by questions of mere fact. The telephone book is full of facts, but it hasn't got enough Truth in it to move an amoeba. Write a Truthful novel—one packed full of your own ragged hurts, joys, fears, passions, rage, love—and you'll have a book that can move mountains. Rip open your chest and yank out the naked Truth and show it to the whole world and you just might be a novelist.

~Randall Ingermanson, author of *Double Vision* (Bethany House).

*   *   *

The most valuable lesson I've learned about writing is that you have to sit down and do it. Every day. Well, almost every day. Even when you don't feel like it. Paragraphs don't get written, ideas don't get turned into stories, or stories into books until the words are on a page. And that doesn't happen until you sit down and write.

~Roxanne Henke, author of *After Anne* (Harvest House).

*   *   *

The most valuable lesson I've learned about writing is that Ernest Hemingway was absolutely correct when he said that every writer needs a "built-in, shock-proof, *manure* detector." Ernest actually used a pithier term, but his point is what matters: writers need the ability to evaluate the quality of their own writing. Writers lacking such equipment make two kinds of mistakes—both equally destructive. One the one hand, they may conclude that their initial drafts are ready to be published. And so, they don't do the rewriting and fine-tuning that is an essential part of the writing process. On the other hand, they may never be happy with what they've written. They fall into the trap of endlessly rewriting their words, thus never finishing anything they begin. The best way I know to develop a well balanced "quality detector" is to read lots of books with an eye toward understanding what each writer was trying to accomplish. In time, you become increasingly able to judge your own words.

~Ron Benrey, co-author of *Dead as a Scone* (Barbour Publishing).

*   *   *

The most valuable lesson I've learned about writing is to give my talent to God. Then seek His help with it daily. He created my gift of writing in the first place. He knows better than anyone, including me, how it can best be used.

~Brandilyn Collins, author of *Brink of Death* (Zondervan).

*   *   *

The most valuable lesson I've learned about writing is that marketable creativity demands discipline. And discipline will see me through even those times when my passion wanes and a deadline looms. Just as a runner learns to pace himself in a race, I've learned to keep pushing, knowing that I'm headed in the right direction and will eventually get a second wind—that exhilarating feeling that I'm being carried by something (and Someone!) bigger than I am, and there's no stopping me.

~Kathy Herman, author of the Baxter Series (Multnomah).

* * *

I've learned two major lessons, after a quarter of a century earning my living as a writer (yes, I'm a slow learner):

#1 Take your writing seriously. God hasn't given you your gift just so you can say you're a writer. Writing is a ministry, a responsibility, a testimony. Books that come from Christian writers should have the reputation of literary excellence in the world. We have the best Creator living in our hearts and marrow; our work should reflect that quality. Don't settle for publication. Press on to excellence that pleases the Giver.

#2 Don't take your writing so seriously. God's in control of your career, whether you sell millions or whether nobody but your mom ever reads your book. Rewrite like crazy, but your prose will never be perfect, may never be as great as you want it to be. Rejections aren't the end of the world; they just feel like that. Realize that your talent is "under construction," in the same way your life is. God will pick up the slack.

~Dandi Daley Mackall, author of *Love Rules!* (Tyndale House).

* * *

The most important thing I've learned is that persistence and hard work are more important than talent. Talent is a gift, but if it is kept in a box under the bed, it's useless. Many more talented people than I am will never be published because they will never do the work required. I love the idea stage of a novel, that misty place in my imagination where the next book promises to be perfect, the best thing ever written. I love typing *The End* and the relief of knowing I am finally finished. Everything else is hard work.

~Robin Lee Hatcher, author of *Beyond the Shadows* (Tyndale House).

* * *

The most valuable lesson I've learned about writing is to go with it and have fun! Yes, it's hard work. Yes, you have to force yourself to sit there, day after day after day all by yourself at your computer. But writing fiction is so much FUN. It's like being a child and staying home from school and sitting on your bed and playing with hundreds of imaginary friends. My late mother-in-law used to see us straining and laboring to do a job she would say, 'you're making such

heavy work of it.' Whenever I find myself straining and laboring and crying over a story that won't come together, I remember her words to 'lighten up.'
~Linda Hall, author of *Chat Room* (Multnomah).

*   *   *

The most important lesson I've learned about writing is that it is like my faith journey—I'm always learning. After completing seventeen books, I'm still discovering while I'm creating. In fact, there are times I can feel like I know less than when I started so I find many ways to learn. Reading books by writers who say it better than me, listening to other writers no matter their level of expertise, and praying my way through each and every book, struggling to make that book not a *good* book but my *best* book.
~Carolyne Aarsen, author of *A Silence in the Heart*, (Steeple Hill/Love Inspired).

*   *   *

The most valuable lesson I learned is that my identity cannot come from my successes and failures as a writer, it flows from knowing I am a dearly loved child of God. In practical terms, this means that there is no correlation between my rank on Amazon.com and my value as a writer and human being.
~Sharon Dunn, author of *Sassy Cinderella and the Valiant Vigilante* (Kregel Publications).

*   *   *

When I was in college—back in the dark ages—a professor told me I couldn't write anything truly meaningful because what I wrote was "too senti-mental." It took me many years to overcome that negative pronouncement and to realize how very wrong he was. What he should have told me, and what I advise other struggling writers, is to write from your heart. I once heard that writers write to figure out what they believe. Thus for each of us, writing from one's heart will mean something different and each of us must discover what it means for us. Writing from the heart means getting in touch with our own feelings; it means looking for our story-telling soul. Writing from the heart is imbuing your work with your very own distinctive view of the world. Writing without heart is spiritually barren—the work won't touch people, and if it doesn't touch an editor somewhere, it will never be bought. I venture to guess that for most of us, knowing our heart comes as a result of a journey to find our authentic and unique voice, our authentic selves. And as many artists and writers will tell you, this knowledge only comes with our willingness to be vulnerable, to let the story find us and control us instead of the other way around. This is by far the most important thing I have learned as a writer.

~Carol Umberger, author of the Scottish Crown Series (Integrity Publishers).

*   *   *

The most important thing I've learned (am learning) about writing is *balance*. Like not taking myself or my writing too seriously while understanding the need to be serious about my writing. It's caring about my readers but knowing I can't please them all. It's reading great writing without getting discouraged over my own shortcomings. It's about pushing myself hard but giving myself grace, and knowing when it's time to work and when it's time to play. It's all about balance.

~Melody Carlson, author of *Finding Alice* (WaterBrook Press).

*   *   *

The most valuable lesson I've learned about writing is…get a therapist! Well, have available a best friend and praying people, maybe that therapist too. Then give the story your creative heart, soul and mind—all that's within you.

~Cindy Martinusen, author of *The Salt Garden* (Tyndale House).

*   *   *

The most important thing I've learned about writing is that, to write well, you need to read well. Constantly. Writing fiction well is almost impossible. There are so many ways to get it wrong. But there's good news. Writers who have gone before you have figured it out. Read what they've written and learn from them. And don't give up. Keep at it. God gave you the ability to write, but you have to take that gift and make it your own.

~Janet Benrey, co-author of the Pippa Hunnechurch Mysteries (Broadman and Holman Publishers).

*   *   *

The most important thing I've learned about writing is surrender. When I try to control the process, forcing myself into a quota or project without the passion and joy to support it, I get dry; my writing doesn't sing. When I try to take control of sales or marketing or promotion, my creativity dies. When I write what I want instead of staying in tune with what God wants, it becomes a human effort. Only by surrendering the call, by laying my desires at the cross, can I find the divine Muse and accomplish my mission. It's very freeing.

~Kristen Heitzmann, author of *Secrets* (Bethany House).

*   *   *

The most valuable learned is to stop panicking and start enjoying what I do. I started out as an anxious writer feeling as though this was going to be one of those claw-your-way-to-the-top kinds of careers. But as the years pass, I've come to realize that stopping to hear my son play a new guitar riff is not going to affect the outcome of whether or not a reader is going to enjoy my stories. If I'm not living my life fully then I'll not have a thing in the world to write about. So I simply live it, taking walks in the sunshine and the rain and telling the stories that I learn whether under sun, moon, or cloud.

~Patricia Hickman, author of *Nazareth's Song* (Warner Faith).

*   *   *

The most valuable lesson I've learned about writing is to enjoy every moment of it. Every blood-sucking, beat-your-head-against-the-wall, I'm-the-worst-writer-ever moment. Those hallelujah, I'm-quite-possibly-brilliant moments are great, too. I've learned to try my best to relax and enjoy the process. One day it might all vanish, but right now it's here and waiting for me—a gift from God. And I've learned to never abandon my vision.

~Rene Gutteridge, author of *Boo Who* (WaterBrook Press)

*   *   *

The most valuable lesson I've learned?
That one's easy…faith!
Nothing is scarier than staring at a blank screen. I'm willing to bet that's why there are so many novelists suffering from substance abuse. But each day

of stepping out in faith and seeing God's trustworthiness is breathtaking. Particularly for someone like myself who is language impaired, never read books as a kid, never wanted to be writer, and who was certain such things were impossible. For me writing is a perfect testimony of being able to "do all things through Jesus Christ who strengthens me."

~Bill Myers, author of *Soul Tracker* (Zondervan).

*   *   *

The most valuable lesson I've learned about writing is to avoid reading reviews, good or bad. Bad reviews can cut to the quick, especially when it's clear the reviewer just doesn't get what the writer is doing. Good reviews are great and to be appreciated, but even those can skew your focus, making you look more at self than what truly matters: the One who called you to write. It's not about reviews; it's about writing the best story you can as an offering to the Master Storyteller. So I work to keep my eyes on Him, and let the reviews fall where they may. And any time I want to know whether or not my books are touching people's lives, all I have to do is pull out the letters from those who've read them. Those mean more than any review ever could.

~Karen Ball, author of *Shattered Justice* (Multnomah).

*   *   *

The most important thing I've learned about writing fiction is that no matter how much you layer and nuance, mask and clothe your characters, they will always leave you just a little bit naked on the page. Be prepared. And don't forget the joy. If you're going to be exposed by this life, might as well do a little dance and enjoy it!

~Annie Jones, author of *Mom Over Miami* (Steeple Hill).

*   *   *

The most valuable lesson I've learned about writing is that the best way to learn how to write a novel is to write a novel. Even if you have plenty of writing talent and training, you still need to write some "throwaway" novels in order to learn the craft. So decide that those first few books are simply a learning experience and don't waste time trying to get them published once they're done. Learn. Practice. Write. Read. Take classes. Write. Join critique groups. Get input. Write. Then, finally, when you write a novel that is so good that everyone who reads it says they couldn't put it down and it simply *must* be published, only then should you turn your efforts toward publication. Anything else and you're wasting time trying to sell rather than perfecting your craft.

~Mindy Starns Clark, author of *The Buck Stops Here* (Harvest House).

*   *   *

The most valuable lesson I've learned as a writer is to think of what I do as a ministry, not a career. If I approach it as a career, then I'm focused on myself; I worry about bestseller lists and critic's reviews and numbers of sales. But when I began to think of what I do as a ministry, I focus on God. He's my "boss" and I give Him my very best, each and every day, disciplining my time, honing my craft—for Him. In return, He provides me with my material needs, just as He provides for anyone whose work is a ministry and not for material gain. Seeing my writing as a ministry also helps me remember that what happens to my book after I type "the end" is in His hands. He will see to it that it gets into the hands of those readers who need it. And when my ministry as a writer is finished and the books no longer sell, He'll give me a new job in His kingdom.

~Lynn Austin, author of *Gods and Kings* (Bethany House).

*   *   *

The most important thing I learned about writing: every writer experiences seasons. There's the heady Spring Season when everything you write gets published and it's all fresh, new, exciting. There's the Summer Season full of readers, fans, people who recognize your name, and the promise of unending future contracts. There's the Autumn Season when prospects become sparse and you need encouragement to stay productive while you rethink who you are and where you're headed. Then there's Winter Season's icy lulls of waiting and wondering if it's all over and that's all you've wrote forevermore. The neat thing about it—winter doesn't last if you keep plodding with that next idea.

~Janet Chester Bly, author of *Words To Live By For Women* (Bethany House).

*   *   *

The most valuable lesson I learned about writing is that when the plot drags, shoot someone.

~Stephen Bly, author of *Paperback Writer* (Broadman & Holman).

*　　*　　*

The most important thing I've learned about writing is that the joy of the Lord really is my strength. When the joy isn't there, I'm empty. The books that are still selling are the ones told when my heart was full.
~Robin Jones Gunn, author of *Sisterchicks Down Under* (Multnomah).

*　　*　　*

The most valuable lesson I've learned as a writer is to forget the point and write the story. If I concentrate on my characters and the trials they go through, the theme develops on its own.
~Donita Kathleen Paul, author of *DragonQuest* (WaterBrook Press).

*　　*　　*

The most valuable lesson I've learned as a writer is that my only goal is to be faithful to the One who calls me. I can't control results, reactions, reviews, or sales. But I can be faithful. This is particularly helpful in the middle of a project when the passion fades and the "how could I possibly think that I could do this?" begins. Then the call to faithfulness upholds me. And that's good enough for me.
~Marlo Schalesky, author of *Only the Wind Remembers* (Moody Publishers).

*　　*　　*

The most valuable lesson I've learned about writing is that I can't write. I had a good laugh with God about that, since I believe He's the One who called me to it. So, what I had to do was go through the hard, torturous work of learning the craft, and still am, plus relying heavily on God.
~Sylvia Bambola, author of *Waters of Marah* (Moody).

*　　*　　*

Listen carefully to what other authors, editors and marketing representatives tell you; filter that information through prayer, and then write the words

God gives you. Make it your heart's desire to please Him and not the world. Oh, yes—and be prepared for criticism and rejection along the way.

Judith Miller, co-author of *A Love Woven True* (Bethany House).

*   *   *

The most important thing I've learned about writing is that I am not writing for myself—that is called *journaling*. I write for readers who spend dwindling discretionary time and money in my company. Customer service isn't just for restaurants and retail, it's for writers. As a professional I do what I must to provide an exciting and satisfying read; as I honor my readers and the Lord, my work will soar.

~Sandra Byrd, author of *Friends For a Season* (Baker/Bethany House).

*   *   *

The most important thing I've learned is to write from my passion. I can write many things, but writing from my deepest passions creates the best stories. To know that God has placed that passion in my heart in order for me to do something about it—no one else can write it quite like me. And to always, always continue to read excellent books and develop my craft.

~Lissa Halls Johnson, author of *Bad Girl Days* (Focus on the Family with Tyndale House Publishers).

*   *   *

The most important thing I've learned is that all the other important things I've learned don't mean anything if I don't add hard work to my knowledge and actually produce a book.

~DeAnna Julie Dodson, author of *In Honor Bound* (Crossway Books).

*   *   *

The most valuable lesson I've learned about writing is to devote large blocks of time, on a daily basis, to improving my sentences. What I have on the page now is Silly Putty; it must be stretched and molded and added to, all in an effort to make it appear, in its final form, as original and seamless. So learn to love sentences. For with good sentences one can build paragraphs, and with good paragraphs, chapters, and with good chapters, books. Anne Lamott said it best: "Writing is like driving at night—the headlights only show the next few feet of road, but you can make the journey that way."

Hone your craft, trust your God, and get it done.

~Ray Blackston, author of *Flabbergasted* (Revell).

*   *   *

The most valuable lesson I've learned about writing is that it's not about me. It's about Him. It's a lesson that I'm constantly relearning—what I write will affect people. I try and keep that as a reminder so that the words on the page will in someway challenge people to a closer walk with Jesus.

Clay Jacobsen, author of *Interview with the Devil* (Promise Press).

*   *   *

The most valuable lesson I've learned was my answer to an aspiring writer who asked, "Does it just flow through you?" I understood the question because after God so dramatically called me into writing, when I had no idea I could be one of "them," I thought it would be easy and the natural results would be fame and fortune. I appreciate God's not letting it just flow through me. The learning and struggle have been worthwhile. I have learned, grown, tried, failed, cried, prayed, enjoyed, delighted in and experienced innumerable emotions while creating my stories and learning the craft. God and I are in this together. I can't write without him. He won't write my books without me. I love the combination.

~Yvonne Lehman, author of *Coffee Rings* (Barbour).

*   *   *

The most valuable lesson I've learned about writing is the absolute need for courage. Courage to face the blank page. Courage to mine the depths of my own pain and passion, to lay bare the frayed tapestry of my life for others to see. Courage to write from within my character's storehouses of love...and hate, joy...and suffering and to immerse my mind in a viewpoint opposite my own. Courage to let a first-reader see an immature manuscript, to let an editor read a first-draft, to let a reader hold the final product with the freedom to enjoy it or set it aside. Courage to trust God's sovereignty through manuscript rejection or the scathing critique of a review, and finally, the courage to give God the credit when the words come out just right. Without courage, our books may entertain, but will not inspire, they may be read, but not reread, they may be liked, but not treasured. Writing that flows from a heart of courage captures the chance to offer our readers more than an escape from life's misery; it gives them what they need most of all: courage to take another step. And another. And then another. We may as well enter the battlefield without armor, in naked embarrassment, than to take up pen or keyboard without courage. To arms, fellow writer. Cast off passionless technical exercise. Summon courage. The page awaits!

~Harry Kraus, author of *Could I Have This Dance?* (Zondervan).

*   *   *

One of the most important things I've learned about writing is the need to keep it fun. Perseverance and professionalism are necessary, but without enjoyment and pleasure in the process, the words on the page often lack the spark of life. Work at keeping writing fun by adopting a perspective that rejects self-importance and seeks the joy of the Lord in the journey.

~Robert Whitlow, author of *The List* (WestBow Press).

*   *   *

Writing is like the adage: we are what we eat. What goes into the imagination determines what comes out. If I dine on rich ideas, consume great truths, savor beauty, and fill my life with an array of unforgettable characters, the stories just seem to flow. I think God expects us to live large and listen well. "Taste and see..."

~Wendy Lawton, author of *Shadow of His Hand* (Moody Publishers).

*   *   *

My most valuable lesson is that it's not my job to write the great American novel or to get Oprah to know my name or to win an award. It's my job to show up, to assume the position of a writer and to tell the story that I've been given the best way I know how and to trust that I'm not alone in the telling. The other valuable lesson comes from Anne Lamont's book *Bird by Bird* and it's the quote "You don't have time for that" that I keep at the top of my computer to help silence the harpies that live in my head and keep me from remembering the first lesson.

~Jane Kirkpatrick, author of *A Land of Sheltered Promise* (WaterBrook Press).

⋆   ⋆   ⋆

The most valuable lesson I have learned about writing is that when I choose a subject about which I am passionate, it is a healing, exhilarating experience.
~Peggy Darty, author of *When the Sandpiper Calls* (WaterBrook Press).

⋆   ⋆   ⋆

The most valuable lesson I've learned about writing is that it's first about healing, accepting, respecting, loving, and forgiving...myself. The second-most valuable lesson I've learned about writing is to go for the heart: His, mine, and the readers'.
~Anne de Graaf, author of *Into the Nevernight* (Tyndale House Publishers).

⋆   ⋆   ⋆

The most important thing I've learned about writing is that everybody has a story. (Even me!) Sounds simplistic, I know, but that's what I tell kids when I speak at schools around the country. That storytelling isn't rocket science, but just a natural way to connect with people no matter what their background. You mean, I didn't have to be rich and famous and ultra-talented to be an author? How about that! Everyone loves a good story, from kids to great-grandparents. And as a Christian, I have a special opportunity to share my hope with heaven-flavored creativity. That's a pretty exciting line of work to be mixed up in!
~Robert Elmer, author of *The Celebrity* (WaterBrook Press).

⋆   ⋆   ⋆

The most valuable thing I've learned about writing is that you never "arrive." There will always be rejections, but it's not a reflection of you person-ally. There's always something new to learn, some way that you can take your writing to a new level. The thrill of discovering a new way to portray emotion and character makes each day fresh. Always be reading a book on craft, and you'll never lose the wonder of writing your passion.
~Colleen Coble, author of the Aloha Reef series (WestBow Press).

*   *   *

The five most valuable lessons I've learned about writing are:

1. "Be focused." In my early years, I drifted along, writing whenever I felt like it, occasionally getting published, but achieving very little. I finally realized that I needed to set ambitious goals, then focus intensely on achieving those goals. That realization changed my life and enabled me to become a fulltime writer.

2. "Write daily." There is no substitute for good writing habits. I didn't become the writer I wanted to be until I disciplined myself to write every day.

3. "Write quickly." I was surprised to learn that the faster I write, the better I write. My work has more cohesion and energy when I get "into the flow."

4. "Finish what you start." I used to abandon half-finished writing projects because I got blocked or bored or I got excited about some new idea. I finally figured out that I didn't learn anything by quitting. Only by persevering through problems and obstacles can we acquire new skills and master our craft.

5. "Serve God." Approach writing as a holy calling, not merely a career. God gives each of us a unique message and a distinctive style of communicating that message. If God has called you to write, then serve Him with diligence and humility. As God told Jeremiah, "Take a book and write in it all the words which I have said to you..." (Jeremiah 36:2).

~Jim Denney, author of the Timebenders series (Tommy Nelson).

*   *   *

The secret to any Christian writing is the three P's: prayer, persistence, and patience. Of course writing ability helps a lot too, but many talented writers never reach their potential because they can't accept the reality of the three P's.

Everyone readily agrees with prayer. They'd sound like a bum believer if they didn't. But perseverance and patience are different. They're hard. They require a level of commitment to both the Lord and the craft that can be painful.

Many seem to think that if God wants you to be a writer, then, kaboom! Wonderful things happen immediately. Publishers fight over you. Your books sell great numbers. Fame and fortune (to be used for the Lord, of course) follow.

Bunk. Phooey. Fiddlesticks. Reality is that it takes all three P's—prayer, perseverance, and patience—in whatever proportions the Lord asks.

~Gayle Roper, author of *Winter Winds* (Multnomah).

*   *   *

The most valuable lesson I've learned as a writer is to find your own voice. Yes, learn from others, listen to the masters, but don't try to copy someone else's success. Don't work too hard to be "different," either. It will be forced. Find the writer's voice within and write the book only you can write.

~Neta Jackson, author of The Yada Yada Prayer Group novels (Integrity Publishers).

*   *   *

The most valuable thing I've learned about writing is that I have to live life if I want to write about it. I can't write honestly about life by holing up in my office, banging away at my keyboard, and living in my imagination from deadline to deadline. I have to get into the world and get my hands dirty, love and get hurt, hope and be crushed, dream and be disappointed...I have to know grief and despair, joy and anticipation, pride and humility, frustration and satisfaction, pain and relief, in order to write characters who experience those things. I have to do the dishes, drive the carpool, wash the clothes...I have to be a friend, a mother, a wife, a teacher, a mentor. Only then can I be a writer who can get to the heart of the human condition, and offer something valuable and real to my readers.

~Terri Blackstock, author of the Cape Refuge Series (Zondervan).

All royalties from the sale of this book are going to Samaritan's Purse, a Christian international relief organization. For more information on Samaritan's Purse, visit their web page at www.samaritanspurse.org.

0-595-34113-6

Printed in the United States
103430LV00006B/160/A